Secret City, U.S.A.

AMONG OTHER BOOKS BY FELICE HOLMAN

At the Top of My Voice and Other Poems

Slake's Limbo

The Murderer

The Drac: French Tales of Dragons and Demons
(with Nanine Valen)

Professor Diggins' Dragons

The Blackmail Machine

The Cricket Winter

The Wild Children

The Song in My Head

Terrible Jane

I Hear You Smiling and Other Poems

The Escape of the Giant Hogstalk

Secret City, U.S.A.

FELICE HOLMAN

CHARLES SCRIBNER'S SONS
NEW YORK

This novel is a work of fiction. Names, characters, places, and incidents are either the product of the author's imagination or are used fictitiously. Any resemblance to actual persons living or dead, events, or locales is entirely coincidental.

Charles Scribner's Sons Books for Young Readers
Macmillan Publishing Company
866 Third Avenue, New York, New York 10022
Collier Macmillan Canada, Inc.

Printed in the United States of America
First Edition   10   9   8   7   6   5   4   3   2   1

Library of Congress Cataloging-in-Publication Data
Holman, Felice.
Secret City, U.S.A. / Felice Holman. —1st ed.   p.   cm.
Summary: Against all odds, Benno and his friends in the ghetto turn an abandoned house into a shelter for the homeless.
[1. Dwellings—Fiction.   2. Homeless persons—Fiction.
3. Poor—Fiction.   4. City and town life—Fiction.]
I. Title.   II. Title: Secret City, USA.
PZ7.H7325Se   1990   [Fic]—dc20
ISBN 0-684-19168-7   89-39841   CIP   AC

For
my much-loved grandsons,
Ari and Adam,
and their world

Secret City, U.S.A.

one

In Cities, the edges sometimes die or sometimes the very centers die, spreading decay toward the edges. And while that is happening, the people who still live there may toss in their beds, turn sick, and wither. But then there are some who hope to find a way out and sometimes a few who may find a way to make the City live again.

*B*enno takes the stairs two steps at a time in a dash for the roof. When he sprints like this, it is as if he were being chased by wild animals. But he is not being chased. He is being led by his own desire, his desperate need to be alone. Someone may stop him if he doesn't make it to the roof in a few seconds. Someone will call his name, command his attention, take him over. One flight, two, three, and he is there. It is *his* space—his and the pigeons'. In summer he may even sleep there, just to get away from the heat, the noise, the smells of the apartment on the second floor of this tenement where he lives with his family.

1

Now he is at the door to the roof. It sticks. He leans on it, gives it a frantic bang, and the bats in the stairwell flutter in their sleep. Then he kicks it with his sneakered foot and the door springs open, catapulting him to his hands and knees on the gritty tar-papered surface. He breathes deeply, gulping the cold, sunny, March air.

JoJo, his old grandfather, died two nights ago: JoJo, the heart of the family, Benno's friend since he was born, died as apologetically as he had lived. Sorry. Sorry to be so much trouble. Sorry. And since then Benno has been seized by the need to stop whatever he is doing, leave whomever he is with, and run for the quiet, leaving the family to deal with everything that is going on: deal with the funeral arrangements, deal with their neighbors coming to weep, and yes, deal with the new empty space in the crowded apartment—a space you notice in its emptiness and want to cry about when you see.

From the roof Benno can see everything in his entire world. He squints and pretends it is a movie. Below him, the streets are jammed with people. As far as he can see this is so, as if the passing winter has released them all from a spell or from hibernation and they have once again flocked to the streets to test the sun. In the distance to the south the high spires of downtown glitter: a place of steel and glass where the rich folks live and work. Benno has been there a few times, riding in the front seat of a taxi driven by Tio Chico, uncle of his best friend, Moon. It is nothing like up here. Nothing like.

To the north are only the flat black roofs, broken chimneys, and wisps of constant fires that smoulder in the empty, wasted houses, deserted by their owners and tenants, one derelict building or another burning all the time. Others stand naked in their bones, waiting. . . .

It is so clear to Benno, when he stands on the roof and sees the city, that people have made an awful mess. They have got too many people too close together and they are always fighting with each other, or cheating each other, or selling each other rotten stuff, or stealing laundry from clotheslines, food or drink from stores, radios from windowsills. Everyone is in everyone's way.

"If I was a king," he once said to his friend Moon, "I wouldn' 'llow stuff like that goin' on."

"Yeah, but we ain't got no king in this U.S.A.," Moon said. "Ya gonna be anythin', ya gonna be like a president."

"Okay," Benno said, moving past the interruption in his train of thought. "Okay, if I was a president, first thing I do is fix up these dumps where we live, make 'em clean wit room fer ev'yone. Gonna be a bat'room in each apartmen', 'stead of jus' inna hall. An' . . . ."

He had lots of ideas: The gangs and kids that did all the rotten things would be sent somewhere to learn to do something good so maybe they wouldn't do all this beating up and ripping off and shooting up and knifing. And then he would make ten minutes of every hour for quiet. Whatever you were doing, you'd have to shut up. His friend Moon says that Benno's ideas are like a dictator's, trying to make people do things like that, even if it is good stuff.

"You can' tell people they gotta shut up," Moon told Benno.

"Why not?" Benno asked. "They make us shut up in school, don' they?"

Moon agreed that was true.

"So, how's that differnt?"

"It jus' is," Moon said. "I don' know why."

3

*   *   *

Benno had often thought about how this city must have been back when the first explorers came here, and then the idea of being an explorer in a new land had seemed so intriguing that he studied the atlas in school to see if there still might be some empty places that he could hope to explore one day. But even though there may be some, they are so far away that now, when he has a hard time even getting subway fare, he can find no real hope inside him that he might go to distant places.

Still, the enchanting image persists—the city, a wilderness, empty of all but Indians, then a few settlers in small huts, then houses, people on horseback, traders and pioneers breaking trails—even on this very street way uptown where Benno now lives sandwiched between other identical tenements, all lined with fire escapes. This was all woodland and fields many years ago. He knows that. Some old men even saw it that way and they told him so. Lots of space. But now everything is compressed, the tall buildings jammed together by some force that squeezes them taller and taller because there is no room for them to be built wider. And in the subway it is the same: the people standing like columns, pushed together by the same force that holds them frozen during their ride.

Now those images fade and the movie of his mind slows down. The people on the street move in flowing slow motion; the sound is turned down; the cars make no sound; the pigeons are suspended motionless in midair. He can do that for an instant—stop the clamor—but it starts again and he is no longer in control.

Beneath his feet is the tenement in which he lives and in which, if things go on like this, he will end his days

4

just like old JoJo did two nights ago—poor, disappointed, embarrassed that he came to this new land to bring fortune, comfort, and pride to his family, and died giving them barely enough to survive, crushed together like this building, like the roaches. He sees and hears a guy named Hot Shot snaking his way through the people on the street below, a large black and blaring radio hefted on his shoulder. Benno knows he didn't have that radio yesterday, but this punk cruises around with a knife stuck in his sneaker and it's easy for him to grab stuff. Sure enough! Here comes some fat kid puffing as fast as he can, yelling, "Gimme back my box, Hot Shot. Ya hear!"

"Prob'ly it ain't his radio neither," Benno tells the pigeons.

"Benn-o!" Very faintly the sound of his name drifts up to the roof. But he is not sure. He is so used to hearing his name called that he hears it even when nobody is calling. That's what he tells himself, anyway.

Right now with his old grandfather dead, there is a quiet war going on downstairs: Who will get the grandfather's room? JoJo had the room to himself because it was so small and because his hacking cough and snore would have kept anyone else awake all night. Still, it *is* a room and therefore has enormous value as a legacy, even though its smoky window faces the blank wall of another tenement. There is about two feet of space between the buildings where air can come in, and if you stick your head out and crane your neck and look up, you can see the sky. Best of all, it is a room with a door!

True, Benno came up to the roof to get away from the weeping and keening below, but even more, he came because he cannot bear the haggling over the grandfather's

5

room. Four kids and two little bedrooms. His mother and father have one room with the baby, and the other had been JoJo's. His young sister, Rosa, has the sofa in the parlor. His older brother, Jorge, has a hammock that he hangs from two hooks near the front door of the apartment. And Benno himself sleeps in a sleeping bag in a corner of the kitchen. What he would give for that room of JoJo's! Anything he has: one of his meals each day, the cracked compass he found in the gutter, *anything*—though he hasn't much else, so there is not much else to pledge. Yet when they had all started whispering about the room, something froze in him and he hadn't staked a claim at all but had started the run for the roof. Privately, he thinks he hasn't a chance at the room anyway. Jorge is older, Rosa is a girl, and he is just somebody in between without distinct rights.

Now he has to admit he is really hearing his name shouted. "Benno! Come! It is *time*." Time! They mean time to bury old JoJo. He doesn't want it to be that time.

Leaning on the roof wall, he can see his friend Moon snaking his way along the crowded sidewalk. Moon has been his real buddy since fifth grade and now, if they both keep getting passing marks, they'll graduate together and start high school in the fall. He thinks he got Moon to stay in school by telling him over and over that he wasn't dumb like they said. Benno doesn't understand how anyone could be stupid enough to think a really smart person like Moon is dumb. The trouble is that Moon's ma and pa are deaf and Moon grew up not hearing anyone talking around the house, so he didn't talk much either. Maybe that's why he seems dumb. He doesn't talk clearly and loudly, but he sure isn't dumb. Not only that, he can talk with his hands in sign language, like he talks with his ma and pa. Sometimes he signs with his hands even when he's talking regular because he forgets everyone can hear him. He's taught Benno some. It is another quiet thing in a noisy world. It is graceful, like dancing. Sometimes Moon and Benno sign to each other when they don't want anyone else to know what they are saying.

And besides all that, Moon's uncle, Tio Chico, was an acrobat when he was young before he came to this country, and he has taught Moon to walk a tightwire and walk upside down on his hands. Moon can do that just as easily as he can walk upright. In fact, sometimes Moon earns some money that way. He jumps onto the back of a truck, riding it downtown to where the big office buildings are. On a sunny day, when business people are going out to lunch, Moon sometimes does some headstands and other tricky things on the corner and collects some change. Sometimes he collects enough for his family to buy food for days. So go ahead, call him dumb!

"Tio Chico, he quit the acrobat business 'cause he broke his back when he was a kid," Moon told Benno once. "That's why he never growed no taller, so then he got to be a cab driver. He tol' me to learn a trade."

"Like what trade?" Benno asked.

"I dunno," Moon said, standing on his head for practice. "All he says is bein' a acrobat is great when the lights is on, but it ain't no good when the lights is off." That's what Moon's uncle had told him.

Now thinking of Moon's uncle makes Benno think of his grandfather, JoJo, again. Things JoJo has said to him have been going over and over in his head all day. JoJo said once, "I was a boy like you, always wanting to be by myself. Then I would walk in the country in the pastures and see flowers in bloom and see goats and sheep and think about how much I liked being there, just growing enough to eat and keeping the animals."

"So why dint ya do that, JoJo—stay there and farm a little?" Benno would ask, and of course he knew the answer because JoJo had told him all this before.

"Because people like us were often hungry when the crops spoiled or the animals fell ill. People worked very hard and got old when they were still young and they'd curl up like a baby in a womb. It was hard to get the crops to grow in those stony hills. Even so, I thought I would like to be a farmer and stay in the fresh air." JoJo spoke in his own musical language and Benno would answer in English.

"So why dint ya, JoJo?" Benno would ask again because that was part of it, the asking and the telling.

"So then my older brother said he was going to the U.S.A. and he said I should come, so I did. I came and I was a laborer when they built those tall buildings downtown. One dollar a day. I thought that was good pay, then, but . . ." Here, JoJo always shrugged his shoulders and looked puzzled as if he could not understand what had happened to the boy from the country, to the man who built stone walls. How had he come to be an old man with a gimpty leg in a tenement in this enormous city?

"But going to a new place is not a bad thing," JoJo had said. "It is a good thing. But me, all I had to give was my back and my hands, that's all." But Benno knew that there was much much more to JoJo than his back and his hands. There was understanding and patience and, though they never said it, there was . . . love.

When JoJo first came to the U.S.A., people would ask

him his name and he would say, "My name is Jose." But in those days, sometimes people took American names and so they said to him, no, it's better that your name is Joe, and that's what they called him. But sometimes he didn't answer because he forgot they meant him. So he'd keep reminding himself. If someone asked him what his name was, he'd say, "My name is Joe . . . *Joe*." He'd repeat it so he wouldn't forget it. So then, pretty soon everyone started calling him JoJo, and that was his name.

"Benno!" A chorus of shrieks. "Come on! It's *time*!" But this is the time he cannot bear it to be. He hears them on the stairs and jumps up, vaults the parapet to the next roof, scaring the pigeons, which flap aloft and then alight once more. He can hear his sister's singsong "Benno! We *have* to go!" Well, they'll have to go without him. He is not going to watch them put JoJo in the ground. He is *not*!

Life was tight before JoJo died, but JoJo made things less bad. He was disappointed, yes, but he understood his disappointment and sometimes he would make jokes about it. "With me for a grandfather," JoJo would say, "the riches may roll in any day. Wait and see. That's what I'm doing." And JoJo would grab his beret and rush out to buy a share of a lottery ticket and keep hoping that, in the end, he would be able to give his family those things for which he had left the old home—some comfort, some pride, and certainly plenty to eat.

Later, curled up near the chimney of a building two houses away from his, Benno can see that the sun has moved way over to the river and it is beginning to get cold. Now they're putting him in the ground, he thinks.

9

Now they're throwing dirt down into the grave. He cannot bear to think of it.

"How'd ya feel comin' to a strange country?" Benno had asked JoJo many times because it was something he wondered about over and over. And each time JoJo had answered in a little different way, depending on how he felt that day.

"Oh, it was big brave adventure," he had once said. "I was a poor small boy traveling on a big ship." Then he had paused. "You think *you* live in a crowd? You should have seen that boat: People sleeping all over the decks and in the hold with the cargo." Other times he would say, "I was very frightened but very excited. I was excited to think I would be coming somewhere new and that I would *be* someone new."

"And were ya?" Benno had asked, very interested. He would like to be someone new.

JoJo had thought about it and finally said, "No. No. I was the same boy in a different place."

Sometimes Benno would talk with Moon about it. "Would ya have the nerve to go somewheres new like yer ma an' pa done . . . like my grandfather done?"

"Sure," Moon said, with his hands as well as his lips. "Sure, if it was a someplace better."

"So why don' we go downtown, at *least*?" Benno had asked. "It's better downtown."

"Nut," Moon said. "You nut. Ya know yer not goin' nowheres downtown to live. Not in yer life."

"Then out west," Benno persisted. "How come all the people in these dumps don' jus' git up an' move out west? How come not? I seen in a movie, once, how there's miles and miles of land out west. How 'bout up north, like in Alaska? Lotsa land up there. Lots."

10

Moon grinned and gave Benno a sock on the shoulder. "Yer a pioneer," he said. "Yer a pioneer jus' like in the hist'ry book. Ya getcha a wagon an' a horse an' be a pioneer. An' I'm gonna go, too. Okay?"

"Okay," Benno said absently. Okay, but he was thinking that a pioneer might really be another name for an explorer. So maybe he *could* be an explorer.

And in this way Benno and Moon thought their way across many miles, finding paths that would take them away from the block.

"Gonna miss JoJo," Benno said once, "when I go way out west."

"Take 'im along," Moon said.

"Yeah!" And Benno had cheered up. "I think I gonna do that." JoJo'd like that, he had thought. He'd like sitting up there in the first wagon, with his cocky little beret keeping his old bald head warm.

He *would* have liked that, Benno thinks now, from his chimney corner on the roof. And he feels tears as his mind leaps down the five flights and across the city to a patch of ground covered with bare earth. And his tears fall on it.

two

A room, says the dictionary, is "an interior space enclosed or set apart by walls." But that is not complete: What a room must have to be a real room is a door. A room with a door that may be closed and leave a person to himself, if he wishes; that gives him a place where he can hear his thoughts. That's a room. Anyone in this part of the City could tell you that without a dictionary, but most would settle for much less. A real room is a dream.

*B*enno's mother gives him a slap. "Where were you?" she shouts. "Where were you when you should be with your family burying your grandfather? All the time . . . *all the time,* you run away when there is something to do. What'sa matter with you, eh?"

Benno turns red, but he doesn't cry. His mother does not really expect an answer. Now he sees Rosa moving her blankets into JoJo's room. So she has won the terrible battle, the battle that he could not fight. Well, maybe he can sleep on her couch? But his older brother, Jorge, has staked that out and, wrapped in an old army blanket, he is sprawled on the couch in comfort.

"You kin have my hammock," Jorge says benevolently.

Benno says nothing, just goes into the kitchen and climbs into his sleeping bag. There is more space in the flat now JoJo's gone, but it is not good space. Benno suddenly sees that it is not so important just to *have* space: What is more important is what is in the space that you have.

In the morning Benno is the first one up, and he grabs a glass of milk and runs down the tenement stairway and out to the street. Moon is there already, leaning against a lamp post. He is making a cat's cradle with a piece of string. Benno has tried to learn, but his fingers are not as nimble as Moon's and they can't seem to remember the tricky turns that change the shape and patterns of the string. Moon stops when he sees Benno emerging from the building, face drawn in a scowl. The cat's cradle turns back into a common piece of string in only a second.

"Hey, magic!" Moon says as he waves the string in the air, then pushes it into his pocket.

"Let's walk," Benno says.

"Where to?" Moon asks, falling into step beside him.

"Anywheres," Benno replies. "Jus' anywheres but here."

They turn north and walk up an avenue of the barrio lined with small stores with signs in English and Spanish: a pawn shop; a hairdresser; a small bar, now deserted except for two men curled in its doorway; a grocery store. Many of the shops are boarded up, but people live in flats above them. Some of those people can be seen beyond the window starting their day, their voices blending to make one clackety sound something like the sound you get when you twist the dial of the radio. Others are leaning out the window, seeing what kind of a day it is, seeing what has happened on the street since they left it last night.

Even though it is early morning, little knots of people have formed, conniving, dealing, fighting. In the doorways lie many sleeping forms wrapped in rags, newspapers, plastic bags, cardboard. The gutters are lined with sacks of garbage, their contents spilling into the already littered streets. A war is going on among six young toughs. Walking along the street, slowly dragging parcels, some old men and old women are talking to themselves. In the background is the intermittent high-pitched sound of an ambulance, a fire engine, a police car. Early morning in the barrio.

"Whatsamatter?" Moon asks. "You not talkin'?"

"I don' ask you whatsamatter when you not talkin'," Benno snaps, and then he hates himself. He feels embarrassed. That was lousy. Just the way some of the other kids heckle Moon for his silence and his sign talking.

"Forget that, okay?" Benno says. "I dunno, I jus' feel like . . . I dunno."

"Yeah," Moon says. "I know. I feel like that sometimes."

"Hi, Benno!" The call comes from an alley they are passing. A small boy possibly ten years old, pale, scrawny, is sitting on a pile of rags, a blanket thrown over his back. Parcels wrapped in newspaper surround

14

him. His face is a dirty little triangle and his hand, raised in a wave, is as bony as a skeleton's. But the expression is cheerful.

"Hi, Willie," Benno calls, but he keeps walking.

The boy jumps up and sweeps his belongings into the blanket, then runs after them. "Where ya goin'?" he asks.

"Nowheres." Benno prods Moon to walk a little faster.

"Can I come wit ya?"

"Not this time, Willie."

"Why not? Ya let that dummy go wit ya."

Now Benno stops and Willie, who keeps charging along, finds Benno's face right in his.

"Whadya say?"

"I din' say nothin'." Willie backs up.

"That's good," Benno says. "That's real good, 'cause if I hear ya say what I think ya said, I gonna flatten yer face."

"Okay, okay," and Willie makes tracks for his alley.

Moon says, "Ya dint need to do that."

Once again Benno is feeling rotten this morning for things he's done or said. Where does he come off threatening this puny person? He knows in his insides that he wouldn't have done it if the boy had been bigger or with some of the tougher boys whom Benno usually *doesn't* challenge when they say the same thing.

"Yeah, but I was jus' mad."

"How come ya don' want 'im to come wit us? I seen 'im aroun' before. He seem okay."

"'Cause if he come wit me, then he wanna come home wit me. It happen before this. An' my ma, she don' wanna have no couchers in our place on 'ccount of we ain't got no more room. We already got my brother on the couch."

"Yeah," Moon says. "We got a lotta people stayin' wit us, too. Sometime it people my ma and pa know from the deaf school, and sometime my Tio Chico he pick up someone he know and bring 'em home in his taxi. My ma, she go near crazy, but she say what kin ya do. Ya can't throw 'em out inna street. If they make a lotta noise, at least it don' bother her, she say, 'cause she deaf." He laughs. "Right now, we got my aunt and her three kids from the islands. They was sleepin' onna steam grate onna street an' she was 'shamed to tell my ma."

Benno kicks a beer can along the street. Suddenly he gives it such a strong kick that it sails up and over the heads of people who are passing. He grits his teeth and says, "Sometimes I jus' git mad at *myself.*"

For a while they walk without saying anything. More and more of the storefronts they are passing are boarded up, with nobody living above. The rutted streets become more rubbled and potholed; some seem barely passable. Buses do not run here. There seem to be no automobiles except for a few gutted corpses. And it has become much quieter, except for far distant sounds.

There are fewer and fewer people on the streets and finally there are only the two of them and a little man of vague shape that Benno sees walking ahead of them. He is bent; he wears a beret; he limps with his left leg. Benno freezes, then breaks into a run. "JoJo!" he calls. *"JoJo!"* Moon catches up with him.

"You flipped? JoJo ain't here, Benno."

Benno feels ashamed, sheepish. "He wearin' the same dumb hat. I fergit he's dead." He says it again. "Dead."

16

The little man has disappeared and they resume their walk.

Moon is the first to notice. "*Hey, wait a minute!* We don' wanna be up here."

Benno, still shaking loose from the image of JoJo, looks around now. He has been walking without really seeing, though his eyes are open. The boys have crossed from the heavily populated area that surrounds their tenement, a sort of disappearing civilization, and into a no-man's land at the northern end of the city; the place from which Benno often sees smoke rising, when he stands on his rooftop.

In the street where they now stand, more than half the buildings are entirely burned to the ground and the rest are shambled and boarded up. The street is a great trash heap of bricks, stone, bits of rusty metal, corrugated tin, indefinable refuse. *There is not a person to be seen.* Nothing moves. The only sound is the barking of wild dogs. The difference between this street and those they have recently left is enormous. *It is another world!*

"This is a no-good place." Moon's hands fly as he signs the words, as if, spoken, they might be heard by some unseen presence.

"I know," Benno whispers. "Ev'yone know that. I dint notice how far we been walkin'."

"Nobody nor nothin' good come in here," Moon says, edging farther back.

"Yeah," Benno says. "But how come? Somebody live here sometime. How come these buildin's all tumbledown now? How come is that?"

"'Cause they got all run-down, like," Moon answers. "'Cause they got all broke up and the ole landlords they din' wanna fix 'em. 'Cause the big bosses in the city say

17

they gotta be fix or else the people gotta leave. Then the city pull 'em down. Tha's the 'cause."

"How d'ya know all that?"

"How come you ast me if you don' think I know?"

"I was jus' askin' anybody, like."

"Me, I'm the only otherbody here."

"C'mon, Moon, cut the kiddin'. How d'ya know that stuff 'bout this . . . this place?"

"'Cause Tio Chico tol' me, long time ago. He know 'bout everywheres there is in the city on 'ccount of he drive his gypsy cab. Ya wanna know somethin', ya ask 'im."

Benno nods. He can accept that authority. "I dunno, though," he says. "In a way, it don' look so bad. Ya know? It got all this light, like, an' space an' air."

"Who ya kiddin'?" Moon says. "It bad."

"Listen to how quiet," Benno says. "Hey, we got ourself in here now, so c'mon, let's look aroun', like." This is the first interest he has felt in anything since JoJo died.

"I dunno," Moon says, but he follows slowly. "It's sort of spooky wit nobody here. Nothin', nothin' at all."

They are edging up the desolate street now, toward the corner where they can see in all directions. And as far as they can see there is street after street like the one they are on—blackened brick and sooty limestone buildings, boarded up, or mounds of their stones like ancient graves. Fire escapes hang like cobwebs, rubble of all kinds everywhere. And smoke. Smoke in the air and seeping through cracks in the street, as if the whole earth were on fire.

"It's like bombed," Moon says, awed.

"Yeah," says Benno. "Totaled. But listen how ya don'

18

hear no voices." He closes his eyes and throws his head back to better experience it.

Then something moves. "It's a cat, I think," Moon says.

"I think maybe a dog," says Benno. "Where could it live? What could it live on?" But whatever it is, it's gone. And the boys continue to move farther into this wilderness, slowly, with fear and caution, yet irresistibly drawn as if pulled by a magnet or led by an outstretched hand. They follow it into this wasteland until there is scarcely a building or part of a building in sight: nothing but rubble and ashes and the occasional wall or isolated boarded-up wreck. And the sun shines on this landscape in such a way that rays appear to come down directly from a point in the sky to a point in the ground; traceable rays.

"Like the moon," Benno says. "It's like the moon."

"An' I thought our street was a dump!" Moon laughs, and the laugh sounds so different in this vast naked place. The laugh bounces away and spreads over the space. "This mus be the dumpiest dump in the whole city."

"Yeah," Benno says reverently. "Maybe the whole state. Maybe the whole country." He pauses. "Maybe *in the whole world,*" he breathes. "Hey! You an' me, we foun' this!" he says, his voice rising. "We *foun'* this," he says again, seeing how it sounds in the strange dusty air. "We're like explorers. We're the *discoverers* of this place."

"Yeah?" Moon says, testing the truth more than questioning it or affirming it. "Yeah."

"Yeah," says Benno. "We's the discoverers of this country."

19

"Country?" Moon asks. "I don' think this here's some diff'rent country."

"State, then," Benno says. "You an' me we discover this new state."

But Moon will not allow it. "Yer bein' a nut, Benno," he says. "This ain't no new state."

"A city, then," Benno says emphatically. "It sure's a city. Ya kin see that." And he points around the heaps of ruins and tries to direct Moon's attention to his vision. "You an' me is the discoverers of this, this sorta secret city what is right here in this country only nobody else know it 'ceptin' you an' me."

Moon surveys the landscape and considers this. Then he nods. It is a valid claim. He can agree to that. "An' what's the name of this here secret city?" he asks.

What a marvelous thing! Benno cannot believe he has overlooked this one great opportunity of his whole life—to name a city. He does not hesitate. The words roll from his tongue without his pushing them off. "*That's* the name. That's the name—Secret City. Secret City, U.S.A."

three

The corners of City streets are magnets. It's as if the streets all tilt toward their ends and gravity pulls into these corners, held up by street-lamp poles, the merchants of the forbidden business of the city. Here the outlaws traffic in bootlegged merchandise, stolen goods, illegal substances. Here, as money changes hands in such "banks," people buy and sell their present and their future. A slum corner is a trap into which the victim may walk of his own free will . . . and may never leave.

The days without JoJo now begin to melt into each other like one long day. Benno has never missed anyone before . . . not like this, as if some of his life has been ripped off. Yes, sometimes a friend has moved away, but it is a shifting neighborhood; he is used to that. This is different. Sometimes Benno sees it as a great distance between buildings. JoJo is standing on the roof across the street, and Benno is standing on his own roof. And the street grows wider and wider and JoJo's roof gets farther and farther away. In reality, Benno often goes up to the tenement roof and stares up at the sky, and sometimes he cries out loud: "JoJo, ya hear me?" He hopes JoJo is not disappointed in heaven, too, and that he can do whatever he was not able to do here.

"Come back!" Benno sometimes may cry. And then in the next second he thinks, why *should* he come back even if he could? It stinks here. And then he goes down to kick soda cans around the gutter, lobbing them expertly over the feet of street people sitting on the curb, their heads on their knees, bags of their few possessions looped onto their arms.

What would JoJo tell him to do, Benno finds himself thinking. And he answers himself: He would want what he wanted to do himself—to free his family from this tenement life. What a task he set himself! Such a plucky young man from a warm island! Such a big dream for a little man with a gimpty leg!

Much later Benno, looking back on this time, will think of it as "the time between." He will not recall how long a time it was that he went to school daily, stared absently out windows, kicked around the neighborhood alone or with Moon, silently, coming home late to curl into his sleeping bag.

"Where ya been?" his father would ask; and Benno would say, "I dunno," and it would be true.

But then, as the days melt, one magic minute happens, just like that! Suddenly one bright May day Benno stands and yells at the sky, "*I'm* gonna do somethin', JoJo. I am."

And after that it seems as if the space between the

roofs closes up and now it feels as if he and JoJo are on one roof and as if JoJo has not gone away although Benno can't really see him. This affects him as just a warm feeling, a comfortable feeling, so he runs downstairs and into their apartment to sit with his family at supper.

"Where ya been?" his father asks him then.

"On the roof," Benno says, taking a big hunk of bread, dunking it into the chili.

Now that May has come, it is as if the tenements have been turned inside out. Everything and everyone that was on the inside is now on the street. People get the kitchen and parlor chairs and sofa cushions and put them on the steps of the building. The women sit with their arms folded across their chests talking, while their youngest children sit at their feet or crawl up and down the cracked stone steps. At the sides of the stoops, the men, out of work or on welfare, stand in little groups nodding at each other or punching each other out. At the curb, what look like the same homeless old men and women pause with their sacks of possessions to sort through another trash can. At the corners, knots of teenage kids or older boys play cards, smoke, deal in drugs or stolen objects. It is the commerce of the slums.

Smells that issue from the open doorways are those of too many people closed up together for the winter with bad plumbing and often not much cleaning. All the cooking odors still linger and have turned to garbage stinks. Benno thinks it is worse when the warm air heats them than when the winter freezes them. But bad smells are just a part of this life. On the roof, the air is dif-

23

ferent—more smoky with all the chimneys around and even, sometimes, the charred air blown down from the burned-out section to the north of them. But it is easier for Benno to breathe that smoky air than this soup that stalls over the barrio, being recycled and recycled through the lungs of the multitude.

As the day progresses the streets become full of snarling traffic and every half-hour or less a police car comes shrieking into the block and stops to haul a down-and-outer from some hallway, break up a fight between punks, pack a couple of pushers into the backseat, or charge up the stairs to emerge after a while with a shouting man and woman who are shoved into the caged back of the patrol car. The residents who are standing around hardly look up to witness these ordinary events, returning very quickly to their business at hand.

"Let's go," Benno says suddenly to Moon, on this bright May Saturday. They have been bouncing a soft rubber ball off the steps for points. Benno is tired of old Mrs. Gonzales yelling "You kids git outa here" every time the ball comes even close to her.

"Where we goin'?" Moon asks.

"Anywheres," Benno says. And so they start east a little way toward the river, then north. They have been walking a half an hour or so, not talking, when Moon nudges Benno and says, "Hey, ya know where we are?"

"Yeah," Benno says.

"That's where ya want us to go?" Moon asks, nervously.

"Yeah," Benno answers.

"Why? Why ya wanna do that? We was there already."

"'Cause I wanna look at it again." This seems like a good-enough reason to Moon, but "I dunno" would have been a good-enough reason. Moon understands things like that. It has to do with his parents being deaf and him not talking much. He understands meanings, not only words.

But before they reach the edge of the burned-out area, and are still in the run-down streets of boarded-up stores and the occasional house, as they round the corner they come upon a group of gaudy-looking punks leaning on the lamp post, talking something up. Benno and Moon start to fade back into a nearby building, keeping in its shadow, walking easy. No use catching their eyes. But suddenly one of the shave-headed punks lifts his head and sees them. He separates from the group and comes over to them, leaning forward in a menacing posture, as if he might spring. He approaches and puts his scarred face close to theirs. "What ya doin' sneakin' aroun' here, ya pieces of nuttin'? Why ya all scrunched up here at the wall? Who ya list'nin' to?" Benno can see that the letters on his T-shirt spell POISON, and so do all the others'. This guy's voice sounds like sandpaper, and when the boys don't answer, he asks again, grating out, "I ast ya, what ya doin' here?"

"Just walkin'," Benno says. He isn't sure his words made any sound, but they must have because the punk answers.

"Oh, jus' two nice kids out fer a li'l walk, huh?"

"Like that," Moon says very softly.

"Talk louder, I din' hear ya," the punk says, giving Moon a push.

"I say, yeah, we was jus' walkin'!" Moon says loudly.

"Don't ya yell at me!" the punk says, giving Moon a

25

vicious shove. It doesn't matter how many times this kind of thing happens to Moon, he still gets scared to death of these mad-eyed corner kings. "I s'pose yer gonna tell me ya ain't rats fer them He-Devils?"

Benno answers, his voice uneven, "We ain't. Honest, we ain't rats, ner spies, ner gofers, ner nothin' fer no gangs nowheres."

"Yeah? How come's that? Ain't ya smart? Don' ya like money? Don' ya like all the free stuff ya kin smoke or snort?"

Benno wants to tell him he's too smart, that's how come, but he is also too smart to say it. The tough leans down and pulls a knife from his shoe. "See that? Name's Elsie. Elsie cuts up spies. Elsie gonna cut ya up next time I see ya. See that big dude over there?" He points to a very tall, thin, young punk wearing a green feathered hat and silver running shoes. "Tha's Big George. Ya bother Big George, he gonna bother ya like ya don' fergit it 'cause ya ain't gonna have no head to fergit it wit. Ya unnerstan'?" They nod. "Don' lemme see ya aroun' this territory no more." And he pulls his face out of theirs and backs away.

Benno and Moon retreat, too, then turn tail and run around the block. But Benno will not be deterred from his plan. They detour a bit and, taking another approach, they arrive at the edge of the area where the broken-down, burned-out space begins. It isn't that sudden. The last few blocks have been half demolished or burned but with the occasional tenant or squatter, though some might think them uninhabitable. But now there are whole blocks of empty, boarded-up houses, then empty lots. As for the streets, it would be hard to drive a car through them: The roads are that broken up,

26

rutted, and piled with junk. It looks like the city dump. Just in the last street, Benno has seen again the back of the little man with the beret, limping quickly. Once again he starts to call, but stops himself. No, it can't be. And again, when they turn the corner, he is not there. Benno shakes himself as he sometimes does when he is waking up. The experience with the punks scared him, but it's not the first he ever had. Besides, he is excited about this exploration. A surprising feeling comes over him as he takes his first step into the area: A strange wind blows on him; there's a feeling that someone has just taken a heavy pack from his back, an almost joyful feeling that seems unsuited to the barren, wounded landscape.

"We're here," Benno says now. "We're back."

"Yeah," Moon responds. "We're here, but where we at?"

"What d'ya mean?" Benno asks, still moving forward into the wide space, clambering over debris as if arriving on the rocky shore of a desert island.

"Where we at?" Moon repeats reasonably. "What street?" They both look for corner street signs, but the signs have disappeared and the base of a metal post is all that is left.

"What's the difference where we at? We're *here*."

"Okay," Moon says, evenly, "next time you wanna come here, you jus' say to me"—and now he exaggerates his tone—"'Let's you an' me go to 'Here.'" They both laugh. It is the first time today that Benno has laughed. It feels good so he does it again and, since laughter is catching, Moon starts to laugh, too, and they are jumping all over the rubble laughing until their eyes water.

They wander in the new land and pick through the debris, looking, like archeologists, for signs of life, signs of natives who once inhabited these quiet ruins.

"Lookit the place we live," Benno says finally. "Just lookit. Now lookit all this space here. Lookit the space. You kin see the sky from most everywheres. There ain't no trucks. There ain't no junkies. There ain't no people lyin' aroun' the street. There ain't no bad stink. There ain't nobody nor nothin'."

"'Cause it's all broke up an' fallin' down an' burnt out."

"Yeah," Benno says, "but it ain't right that all this space kin be here an' ain't nobody usin' it."

"How they gonna use it?" Moon asks.

They hear a sliding sound and then a bang. They freeze and retreat a bit.

"Someone's here!" Moon says, and crouches low. The sound comes again, then it stops.

"Maybe it's jus' some junk fallin' from one of the walls, like all the resta this junk," Benno says, gesturing at the piles of debris. All the same, they move very cautiously. In the distance they hear the sound of howling dogs.

Now they have come to a street in which two nearly intact buildings still stand near the middle of the block, one sort of leaning on the other. And across the street is another building without its two top floors but which otherwise looks like a real house compared to the other ruins. They walk into the block, picking their way among the broken limbs of a dead civilization.

"Look at this!" Benno exclaims. "Jus' look at this! I noticed there's a few buildin's aroun' that don' look so bad. Like, look at this one."

Benno is pointing to one of the two buildings that appear to be supporting each other, leaning together like two old friends, a bit halt and lame. The windows are boarded up, as is the door. As they move closer they can see that one of the buildings has no back. It seems to be sliced open. But the other looks almost whole. It appears to have been miraculously protected by fate from some disease that started at the corner and worked its way in.

"Let's take a look inside," Benno says.

"I don' think we oughta," Moon says.

Benno proceeds as if he has not heard. He kicks some hunks of concrete from the step with his sneaker, winces, and climbs the dusty, cracked stone stairs to the boarded-up doorway. He tries to peek through the cracks, but he can't see anything except that there is a door behind the boards. He climbs up onto the cracked concrete wall of the stoop and edges over to try to look beyond the boards that cover the window.

"I think I kin see some light in there," he calls.

"Ya mean 'lectric light, like someone's there?" Moon asks nervously. "Ya think someone's there?"

"Nah, I mean like daylight is comin' in there from somewheres. Let's go aroun' the back." And Benno jumps from the low wall onto the stoop and runs down the steps.

Quietly they make their way around one side of the building, climbing over the hunks of concrete and rotted wood that litter the path. Then they are standing in what was once the backyard of this house, though now it is a junk heap, knee deep in debris. They stand regarding the rear elevation. A warm wind blows dust and bits of torn paper and then suddenly a shutter on the second floor opens and then, as they hold their breath, shuts. And again it opens and then shuts. They stand frozen, waiting for someone to appear any moment to challenge them. But all that challenges them is the wind, an entirely different wind, it seems, than the one that blows in their block.

From this side the house seems one floor taller than from the front because of its stoop. The first-floor windows here are small and close to the ground.

"See," Benno says, "the window I was lookin' in, in the front, is on the second floor here."

Moon points upward. "Maybe that's where the light's comin' from." He indicates a long window that has two shutters on it. They must have been nailed shut at some time, like those in front, but one is loose and slowly swings back and forth on its hinges as the strange wind blows it. Now and then it clatters against the house.

"See, so I was lookin' from the front room through to that back window, maybe," Benno says. "I wanna try and git us in there." An unusual sense of the moment grips him.

"Yer crazy!" Moon says. "Ya wanna get us arrested fer breakin' an' enterin'?"

"Ya see anyone aroun' here gonna call the cops?" Benno asks.

"No," Moon admits.

"Okay, then gimme a hand. I *gotta* take a look."

Benno searches the backyard junk for a tool. He picks up a medium-size rock for a hammer, and a rusted piece of pipe.

"Ya gonna try an' open that door?" Moon asks, pointing to the boarded-up back door.

"Nah, I'm gonna look for someplace hidden." Benno

crosses the yard to the splintered steps, then, pulling away rubble, ducks under them and starts to pull debris from around a small wooden window hatch.

"Ya gotta be careful with this junk," Moon says, picking up a piece of rusted pipe that Benno has thrown into the yard.

"I know," Benno says. "Ya kin get tet . . . tet . . . poisoned." And he is careful as he slowly uncovers the little wooden window under the steps.

Benno takes the heavy stone tool and bangs on the piece of pipe he had picked up in the yard. He stops and looks at the end, then hammers it some more until he has flattened it a bit and sharpened it. Then he uses it to try to pry open the window hatch. At first it seems it will not move, but slowly, slowly, it gives way and they are peering into the dark basement floor of the house. A draft of very dank air floats out at them.

"Whew!" Benno says. "It stinks. But the air will fix it some. I'm goin' in," he says. "Ya comin'?"

Moon is reluctant, but he nods. First Benno uses the pipe to whack at cobwebs that block the opened window, then he lowers himself into the house. When his eyes adjust, the dim light from the window illuminates an ordinary basement with an enormous furnace, its flue disconnected and in many pieces, its heavy iron doors ripped off. The floor is littered with cans and broken bits, loops of wire, an old radiator, and myriad odds and ends. There are pipes overhead, some broken and dripping. Under one, a pool of water has spread over one whole side of the basement, making a shallow pool.

Benno signals to Moon with a whistle. "Ya comin'?" and in a minute Moon's legs, body, and finally his head come through the window and he joins Benno.

"Boy, this is near as big as a bowling alley," he says.

"Look, here's the stairway up to that floor we saw from the front," Benno said.

Moon looks. It's dark. "We can't go up there 'cept if we got a flashlight," he says. "Remember how the steps is broke in my house? If'n we break a leg here, nobody ever gonna find us."

"Yeah, I guess," Benno says. "Where we gonna get a flashlight?"

"My Tio Chico," Moon says. "He got some in his cab in case he get stuck at night or somethin'. I'll ask him if'n I can borrow one fer a while."

"Okay, so let's get outa here, then," Benno says. He is in a hurry to get on with this. He wants to see the rest of the house. He wants . . . He isn't sure what he wants but he feels it is very urgent.

They climb out the little window and carefully pile enough lightweight trash in front of it to obscure it. Then they go around to the front of the house again and get their bearings.

"We gotta remember jus' where this place is at," Benno says. "We gotta make some kinda map to show the way we come in." He burrows a bit in the debris near the stoop and finally comes up with a piece of partially burned coal. "I kin write wit this," he says, "but what I gonna write on?"

"Never mind the map," Moon says. "What we kin do is we mark the trail with that piece of coal. Look." And he takes the coal from Benno and reaching way up, marks an X above the boarded doorway of the house. Then he turns and starts toward the corner. At the corner Moon climbs the rubble and makes a small X on the side of a tumble-down wall. Then he adds an arrow pointing into the street the house is on.

"Cool!" Benno says. "But which way did we turn at this corner?"

"I think we come right straight up this street fer a coupla blocks," Moon says.

"Yeah, maybe yer right," Benno says. So they start to retrace their steps, turning and reorienting themselves, marking ruins with X's and arrows, then going back, crossing them out and making new ones as they find they have chosen the wrong route.

It is a long trek, but not as long as the return from their first visit, when they had circled and circled in the newly discovered wasteland, finally guiding themselves even as explorers would, keeping the sun on their right side, knowing that thus they would arrive south of where they were. Now they have found another trick: They keep the sound of barking dogs behind them and the increasing volume of city sounds ahead as they approach the barrio.

There is something else that Benno notices: It is how he feels as he grows closer to the familiar sights and sounds. It is as if in here, in this space, he is wearing different clothes, and as he comes away the clothes change back to his regular stuff. And his voice sounds different, too, in the world outside The Space: maybe rougher, louder. And all over him, it is like he was a different person for a while and now he is back to the way he usually is. He does not mention this to Moon as they return now to the screeches, sirens, and horns; to the familiar sight of people looking down at the sidewalk as they slouch along, as if the answers to their questions were to be found there. And there are the old people

33

and children sorting through the trash cans of the alleys. There is no mistaking that Benno and Moon are back in home territory.

"Ya think ya could get the flashlight by tomorrow an' we could go back to the house in the Secret Ci—" He cannot say that name here, somehow. ". . . In that, uh, space?"

"If'n Tio Chico's at my house an' I kin catch 'im," Moon says.

"See ya, then," Benno says as they reach his building. "See ya in the mornin' an' we go on up to . . . to The Space."

four

In a deserted City, wind can blow through the empty streets as wind has always done in desert ghost towns. There is something about them that invites the wind to blow away the dust of a civilization that has left the place to crumble.

Next morning they are following the X's they had made yesterday for trail markers. Benno is carrying a paper bag with some bread in it. Moon carries a heavy-duty flashlight produced last night by Tio Chico from among several he carries in his cab.

"He ask ya why ya want it?" Benno asks.

"Nah," Moon says. "Tio Chico, he don' ask. Tha's the way he is." Benno considers this. It surprises him. He hardly asks for or does anything that somebody doesn't ask why or what for or where. But sometimes when he is sick of it and he gets mad he says, "Can'tcha lemme be?" And his father yells, "What d'ya want? Ya want yer mama and papa don' care whatcha do?" Then Benno feels bad as well as mad.

Now they have come to a confusion of X's. One was a wrong turn. "I think we go this way," Benno says.

"Okay, we try it, but then we come back here if it ain't right," Moon agrees.

And it is wrong, so they return to the X's and take the other turn. They are paying so much attention to the trail that Benno has failed to notice something. Now he stops. "Jus' a minute," he says, holding up his hand. He closes his eyes and listens. He turns his head so a gust of wind can touch his cheek. Yes, he is right: There is something different in this place that makes him feel transformed. He feels he is without a past, without a history. His mind is free; his feet carry his body without feeling its weight; the silence, punctuated only by the barking of dogs, hypnotizes him, lures him, pulls him. It is like his roof, only much much stronger, better, bigger, and filled with possibility.

Moon, used to silences, is undisturbed by this intermission. Also he is temporarily distracted by a flight of birds, in a perfect V formation, flying directly overhead. He and Benno are not the only living things moving in this direction today. With discomfort, though, he sees four or five dogs, several blocks down to the west, dashing with much barking toward something that is out of Moon's line of vision. They are big dogs, fast dogs, and they do not seem like someone's pets off the leash. He hopes they do not see him. He starts to tell Benno, but Benno interrupts.

"Let's go," he says.

After many changes of direction, they are standing where they want to be—at the end of the street where the house stands. Morning light shines on the X on its door frame like a beacon.

"That's it!" they both say as they start the scramble over the obstacles in the street and make their way through the debris along the route to the back window. Removing the camouflage, they drop into the basement, Moon carrying the flashlight, now lit and illuminating creatures scurrying for the cover of the basement wall.

"Nobody but us been here for a long time," Benno says, pushing aside webs that hang like draperies before them as they approach the stairway. Now Moon shines the light on the bottom step and Benno puts his foot on it, testing, as the light illuminates the holes in his sneakers. The step creaks loudly in the quiet cellar, but it seems strong enough. Benno puts his whole weight on it, and the next and the next, as Moon shines his light past him.

"There's a coupla holes but it seems okay," Benno says, and he beats away more cobwebs. "C'mon." And Moon joins him nervously on the stairway, breathing fast and holding the shaky banister. They are facing a closed door. Moon runs the light over it and shines it directly on the doorknob. It turns, but the door doesn't move. Moon says, "Here, hold this," and shoves the flashlight at Benno. He reaches into his pocket and takes out a plastic card, then slips it into the space between the door and the doorframe. He fools around with it for a few minutes. "This lock ain't moved fer a long long time," he says, but finally he moves it and the door swings part-way open. As it does so it cries like a cat, then stops moving.

The boys look at each other: Who will be first? Benno takes hold of the rusty knob and tries to push the old door open far enough for him to pass. It seems stuck, as if someone were leaning on it. This is a vision that

Benno tussles with as he pushes at the door. Something *is* leaning on the door: the house. Floors and walls are no longer at right angles. This door is stuck on a heaved floor; nothing more sinister than that. And finally, sweating from exertion and a little terror, Benno opens the door enough for them to enter. They are in the house.

Like the basement, the room on the first floor is hung with webs, most of which are deserted like the house. Dust is layered on the floor; windows are shuttered or boarded up, some are broken, and the shards lie on the floor. But at the rear of the room in which they find themselves, those shutters stand a bit open, swinging in the breeze. It helps to orient them.

"That there's the window we seen from the yard," Benno says. "This here gotta be the kitchen. See, here's a sink." He turns the old faucet. Nothing happens. There is no stove or anything else that belongs in a kitchen except a few old doorless cupboards on the wall and a closet with shelves on which stand a few cracked jars. They survey the room, waiting for the fear to pass, quieting their pulses. Again, Benno feels the strange silence, the suspended animation. The place, seen through the dust which is lit by the window, seems otherworldly. It is as if they have walked north into not just another place, but another time. Once there were people living here, Benno thought. They were cooking in this kitchen. Where are they?

Now, released from the spell, they begin to move slowly around the first floor of the old house. A wind has come up and is banging the shutter at the kitchen window. It accompanies their inspection. There is a good-sized room off the kitchen, connected by only an empty door frame. A wall stands naked, denuded of its plaster almost entirely. What little of the wall is left is cracked and crumbling. It is like looking into the skeleton of the house. There is no furniture, but there is a fireplace full of trash. The window of the front room is boarded up.

"See that there window?" Benno says. "Tha's the window I musta looked through to that window in the kitchen." It is a finding, a discovery. And now he sees their footprints in the dust. We *are* like pioneers, he thinks.

They are standing in a small hallway near the front door, but they know they cannot open that door to the outside because they saw the boards blocking it. From this hall a staircase, hung with more webs interwoven with dust, rises to the next floor. They start toward it and then they see there is another closed door in the hallway.

"Let's look in here first," Moon says, and carefully opens the door, which, like the other, sticks and creaks. Here is a large room that runs from the front to the back of the house, with boarded-up windows at both ends. Benno whistles. Moon says, "I never seen a room this big in any house I was ever in."

"Me neither," Benno says. "Ya know what I think? I think this house maybe is not a bunch of li'l apartments like we got, ya know. I think maybe this whole house was fer one family . . . one big family."

"All this space fer one family!" Moon says, thinking it over. "Nah. That's crazy." But in a second he says, "But maybe, yeah." Moon does not argue much. Usually he just says what he thinks and lets it go.

This room has a fireplace, too, full of plaster and debris, slung with cobwebs. And through the encrusted dirt on the floor they can see a fancy pattern in the way the wood is laid.

"You ever seen a floor look like that?" Benno asks Moon. "All in designs like a kinda puzzle."

"Not me," Moon says. "I never. Musta took 'em a long time to do that."

"Let's go up the stairs," Benno says. They go out into the hallway and test the stairway. The railing is missing some sections and the banister is wobbly, but most of the steps are okay except for two that have holes in them. In a minute they are on the second-floor landing, in a narrow hallway off which open several doors, some of which stand ajar. Like the downstairs, all the windows are boarded up, giving little light, but the flashlight reveals that there are three small rooms and one larger one. And there is a bathroom. Benno tries the faucet in the battered, nearly black sink. Nothing. He can see that the pipes to the tub have been disconnected and the faucets are gone. Benno gives the old toilet a mechanical inspection.

"If this toilet had water in it, it could maybe work," he says.

"It got no handle, like," Moon says.

"Let's get outta here," Benno says suddenly, as if there were a timetable he is following.

They return to the hall and walk carefully down the stairs, holding the wobbly bannister, avoiding the steps with the holes. Now, as they resurvey the first room they saw, they can see small rodent tracks in the dust.

"Mice," Benno says.

"Maybe rats, too," Moon says.

"What could they eat here?"

"Maybe the stuff in the walls," Moon says.

"Yeah? Mice and rats, they eat that stuff?"

"I think maybe they eat anythin'," Moon says, "jus' like people. You seen all the bums and the kids and people what live in the street down roun' where we live. They eat outta the garbage cans. Those bars there, they throw out lotsa stuff. I seen 'em do it. Potato chips, some kinda beans, bread. The mice an' rats, they eat there, too. I seen 'em."

"Yeah, I seen 'em, too," Benno says. "That kid, Willie, allus tryin' to come wit us, he eat that stuff, I know. There's a samwich place right there in that alley where we see 'im. Yuck!" And he holds his throat and opens his mouth in a fake convulsion.

"Yeah, yuck," Moon agrees. "But if ya got no other stuff to eat, maybe it ain't so bad."

"Nah," Benno says. "It gotta be bad."

Talking, they have made their way down the cellar stairs and have reached the outside of the cellar window. Benno arranges the debris around the entrance again. The place is beginning to look familiar.

The wind that has been slapping at the shutters is whipping up a small whirlwind of dust. It blows over their footprints, wiping them out. Benno turns to look back at the house and sees the wind pick up his footprint and toss it away.

"Look," he says to Moon. "Like we never was here. Like we dint leave no signs."

But signs have been left in Benno's mind. It is whirling. It is dancing. It is leading him through rubbled streets and avenues, out of The Space and into and through the more familiar clutter of the streets of his own neighborhood. Once again he feels the light-footedness, light-

41

headedness leave him as the graffiti-covered walls of the barrio close in; as the boom-box-laden bodies blare down the sidewalks; as the iron-barred fronts of stores replace the open, rubble-strewn streets of his Secret City.

As usual, Moon honors Benno's silence. There is a great deal to do within his own mind. Once he reaches out to grab Benno as he crosses the street carelessly, nearly being nudged by an exhaust-spuming bus. Moon has this habit because he accompanies his deaf parents when they go around the neighborhood. He is their ears when outlaw trucks make illegal turns or crazies on motorcycles come roaring around a corner.

They turn into Benno's block and Benno seems to awaken. Sounds, sights, smells have reached him. He is back in the perpendicular crush of real life. Now they pass the alley where they saw Willie. He is still there or again there. He is sitting with his back against the wall, an arm over his belongings. His head is down; his eyes are closed; he is sleeping. Benno gets a bad feeling as he passes him. He kicks a beer can. He kicks another. Moon looks at him sidewise. Whatever Benno is thinking, it is clear that he doesn't want to talk about it. In fact, all Benno says when they get to his building is, "See ya."

"See ya," says Moon.

five

*You need to outwit the City—trick it, sneak
around its back, learn its secrets, defy it,
and then grow wise and know that you are
a match for it. That's Street Smart—the
graduation diploma that the City must give
its children.*

*D*uring the next few days Benno becomes a scavenger. He scouts the backyards and trash cans. He is not looking for food: He is looking for useful things. Though he is not exactly sure just what those things are, he knows them when he sees them. By the end of the week he has a collection: one old mop, two worn brooms with broken handles, a badly dented bucket with a hole halfway up, and some shards of soap. He has the shadow of a plan and, as he scavenges, he tries to shape it in his mind before he consults anyone, even Moon.

But at the week's end he seeks out Moon, who has been kept busy with the couchers—his mother's sister from the islands and her children—who have fled from the welfare hotel and are bedding down all over the little

43

apartment. He has been put in charge of the two boys, seven and eight, while their mother tends the baby. He plays ball with them and he shows them around the neighborhood. He teaches them street smarts: Don't challenge anyone who can beat you or run faster than you can. Walk out near the edge of the sidewalk, not near the buildings. Stay away from the big toughs who travel in groups; don't look them in the eye; don't go anywhere with them and don't run any errands for them. Keep your nose out of everybody's business and keep one eye in the back of your head. If you see anything happen, pretend that you don't.

Juan and Paco catch on fast. They know their mother wants to go back to the island they came from, but they want to stay in this city. Anyway, it doesn't matter: She hasn't got the money to leave and has no way to earn a living if she could. Their father split before the baby was born, to try to get a job in another city. Meanwhile Juan and Paco want to learn from their cousin how to keep alive on the streets.

Benno finds Moon showing the kids how to open a fire hydrant and get soaked and cool when summer comes. This gives Benno an idea and he scoots home, returning with his salvage. He puts the bucket under the stream of water and drops the broom and the mop ends into the bucket. He sloshes them around in the torrent, letting grime and filth run out of them and into the gutter and down the sewer drain.

"Whatcha doin' wit all that stuff?" Moon asks.

"Tha's what I wanna talk to ya 'bout."

"Okay, talk."

Benno gives a sidelong glance at the cousins, who are in the gutter, jumping back and forth over the stream.

44

"Maybe later," Benno says. "Come over and we'll talk."

Moon nods as he grabs Paco just as he is about to be swept down the gutter with the strong stream of water. He shows them how to close the hydrant. Some people who had been sitting on the curb when he turned the water on have been throwing him angry looks. Now they settle down again and satisfy themselves with raising puny clenched fists, nothing more. They know that their rights are few, even in the gutter.

When Moon says he is coming over, he is coming over. Benno hangs around his stoop, trying to do the cat's cradle with a piece of string and not managing it for the twentieth time. He is still struggling when Moon appears. He takes the string from Benno and shows him again, right in front of his eyes.

"Yeah!" Benno says. "I think I got it." But he hasn't. The string twists and knots in his hands.

"So what ya got to talk to me 'bout?" Moon asks.

"It's 'bout The Space," Benno says in a low voice, glancing about to see if he has been overheard. "I got a idea . . . a big idea," and his eyes gleam with excitement and he bites his lower lip after he says it.

"Okay," Moon says. "What's the big idea?"

"The big idea," Benno replies, dragging his words out as if he is reluctant to part with them, let the daylight shine on them. "The big idea is to make that house in The Space into a place to live: a secret place to live."

"To live!" Moon says. "Like who fer?"

Benno frowns. "I dunno yet," he says. Is this really true, he asks himself. Does he truly not know his own plan? He does not answer himself.

45

"Anyhow," Moon goes on, the soul of reason, "how ya gonna do that? How ya gonna get water and light? How ya gonna get food? How ya gonna. . . ?"

"I don' know that all yet," Benno replies. "But I been thinkin' 'bout this a whole lot an' what I think is we gotta begin at the beginnin', jus' like in any new land. Only here we gotta do even more: We gotta start wit cleanin' the place up. But we can't do it wit only two people. We need more people we kin trust." Now he comes to the really big question that has been bothering him. "Who kin we trust?"

Moon thinks only a few seconds. "We kin trust my cousins Juan and Paco. They both okay kids. They ain't into nothin' bad. An' they do what I tell 'em."

"Yeah?" Benno says, surprised. "I ain't got nobody does what *I* tell 'em. Seem like ev'ybody tells *me* what to do."

"Like who?" Moon asks.

"Like my ma; like my pa; like my brother; an' even like my kid sister; an' like the teachers an'—"

"Okay," Moon says, "but I bet I know someone who'll do what ya tell 'im."

"Yeah? Who?" Benno is really interested.

"That Willie in the alley," Moon says. "Tha's who. He likes you. He, like, 'mires you."

"Yeah?" Benno says. And then he says it again, even more surprised. "Yeah?"

"Yeah," Moon assures him. "Jus' try 'im. Y'll see."

"Ya gonna go 'long wit this?" Benno asks, just to be sure he's got one ally, though he knows he can expect Moon to agree.

"What we got to lose?" Moon says reasonably.

46

They find Willie glued to the wall of the alley, not far from the dumpster. He is chewing on a piece of what might be pizza, and he is so surprised to see Benno and Moon turn into his alley that he stops chewing.

"Hi, Willie," Benno says.

"Hi," Willie replies, a suspicious look, a frown, and then a cautious look of pleasure crossing his face one after another.

"Wanna come do somethin' wit us?" Benno asks, just as if he always asks Willie to join them.

"Yeah? Yeah, I do!" Willie says, and he jumps up and tosses his scattered belongings into the blanket on which he has been sitting, rolls them into a pack, ties them with a string, and throws the package over his shoulder.

"Don'tcha even wanna know what we gonna do?" Benno asks as they start to move through the crowded street.

"Yeah, but it don' matter." Willie shrugs. "Anythin' I do is better'n what I'm doin'."

"We're goin' to a special place," Benno says. "We found it, me an' Moon."

"Yeah?" Willie says. "How come it's so special?"

"'Cause it's secret," Benno says. "'Cause no people know 'bout it 'ceptin' us two, and then maybe you, and we gonna get Moon's cousins and tha's five people. But firs' ya gotta say if ya kin keep a secret."

"Sure I kin," Willie says. "How ya think I stay alive? Ev'y day I see *ev'ybody* 'n' what they all doin'. I see 'em dealin', I see 'em stealin', an' I seen worse, an' I don' tell *no body*." He stops walking and drops the pack, which is

47

half his size. "Ya think I'm stupid!" And suddenly this small ragged boy's chin juts out proudly.

Somehow this makes Moon laugh, and then Benno laughs, and then Willie joins them in laughing, after first looking from one to the other to be sure they are not laughing at him. And they resume their walk, laughing, stopping to give each other small punches on the shoulder, then walking some more and laughing a lot.

At Moon's block, Moon cuts out and runs inside to get his cousins. "This here's Juan an' this here's Paco," Moon says. "This here's Willie an' ya know Benno. I tol' 'em," he says to Benno. "They comin' along wit us."

"Ya tol' 'em it's a secret?"

"Yeah, they know." He turns to them and talks directly at them. "They know they better not tell *no body,* or else!" He looks serious, but then he grins and gives his cousins each a pat on the back.

"Okay, come on, then," Benno says, taking the lead, picking up his brooms and mops and stooping to grab some newspapers out of a trash can. He looks over his shoulder and beckons them. "Come on," he says again. "Yer gonna see The Space."

With Moon and Benno in the lead, the others follow without questions. The pace is fast. For a moment, Benno feels panic when he sees a guy in a POISON T-shirt ahead, but they are not noticed and pass through the territory undisturbed.

"Hey, what ya doin'?" Moon whispers to Benno. "We turn left here."

"I know," Benno whispers back. "I'm tryin' to mix 'em up."

"What fer?" Moon asks.

48

"I dunno. Jus' till we're sure they okay."

And so it is a zigzag course, making the walk longer, and Paco is panting when they come to the outskirts of The Space.

"Oh, wow!" Willie says. "Wha's this place! This looks like . . . like . . . maybe the moon." He had not commented as they passed the increasingly rubbled streets, the windowless buildings that you could see through. But now they are in the wasteland, the no-man's land that stretches to horizons, and he is awed.

"This here is The Space," Benno says. "Tha's what we call it. It has another name but we ain't tellin' that yet. You wanna talk 'bout this to me an' Moon an' we all jus' walkin' down in our block, you call it The Space. Ya hear?"

Willie nods.

Benno continues to lead them on a circuitous route around excavations and derelict buildings, in and out until they are at the front of the house.

"This is it," Benno says. "This here is our secret buildin'."

The three new recruits suck their breath in.

"Ya mean this here house?" Willie asks, his voice full of awe. "This here house belongs to ya? Nah." He dismisses this as preposterous. "Nah. No way."

"Yeah," Benno says. Then adds, "Sorta."

"Wow!" is all Willie can reply, at first. Then he says, "But where we at?"

"This place, far as ya kin see, is The Space: Tha's all ya hafta know right now."

"Don't aks too many questions," Moon quietly cautions Juan and Paco.

"Okay," Benno says. "Now we goin' in the secret en-

49

trance. But before I take ya, I need ya to swear that nothin' could make ya tell where this is or what we gonna do."

Willie volunteers quickly. "I swear," he says. "Sure, I swear."

"I swear," Juan says.

"Me, too, I swear," Paco says.

Benno thinks about those words. Why does that mean more, he wonders, than just saying it plain, without "I swear"? Is it because saying "I swear" is like they know something bad would happen if they broke the promise? Why is that? Just with words. He has heard his mother say "I swear to God . . ." and he understands that she believes that God is guaranteeing her promise. But these boys are not swearing to anything or anyone except to him, Benno, their leader. He feels that his earlier vision of himself—Benno-the-Explorer, leading these people on a pioneering trek—is now confirmed. Yes, he is the leader.

He shows them the way to the back of the house and then removes the camouflage from the entrance window. As he drops into the basement, he puts the bucket under the big leaking pipe that forms the basement pool. Then he leads them, with Tio Chico's flashlight, through the damp and dark cellar, up the creaking stairs, and into the kitchen, dimly lit through the cracks in the shutters.

He waits for them to take it all in. They are speechless. Finally Willie says, "Boy!" and he drops his pack on the floor. "Oh boy!"

"Wait'll ya see the rest," Moon says, and they start a tour. There is not much talking, just a great many gasps.

"This whole room and not nobody in it!" Paco says. They wander in and out of rooms, quietly, unaccustomed to so much unoccupied space. Then, when Benno thinks they've experienced enough, they all return to the kitchen.

"Okay, now," he announces. "This here's what we're gonna do. First thing, we gonna clean this place up. Right now we only got a few things to work wit. We gotta get more. Now we gonna sweep and mop and get all the spidery webs an' stuff outta here." He goes to the kitchen window, unlatches it, and then, with Willie's help, he forces it open and pushes the flapping shutters back. Now they can look down into the jumbled backyard, and they have an overview of the remains of other buildings, in various states of being. Everywhere they look, great fields of rocks, broken chunks of cement, unimaginable tons of debris form a barren landscape.

Moon has already picked up a broom and started to sweep larger pieces of debris into a pile.

"Fer now," Benno says, "we kin just throw all this junk outta the window an' it kin mix up wit the other junk out there. But later we gonna clean up that yard." In his mind he sees it swept clean as in the vision he has been carrying around all these days. "Ya ain't gonna know this place when we get through."

He disappears down the cellar stairs to see how his bucket is doing. There is enough water in it for now and he moves the other bucket over to catch the drip. When he returns to the kitchen, he puts Juan and Paco to work picking up debris that is too big to sweep. Willie, without direction, is using the other broken broom to try and sweep the filthy drapes of webs hanging from the ceiling, walls, and doorways. They are all sneezing from the dust. Benno has been soaking some ends of soap in the bucket of water and now starts to slosh it around in the places that have been swept, scrubbing hard at clots of mud and grime. The result is streaky, but they can begin to see things they couldn't see before. There is some sort of painted border around the top of the walls: a vine or something. The floor is not black, as it had appeared, but a much scratched and dulled brown-stained wood.

The cleaning goes as if an engine were driving it, energy that could create anything . . . nearly anything. Benno dumps what's left in the water bucket out the window, then runs down the cellar stairs and replaces it with the partly filled second bucket. Moon moves his sweeping into the room across the front hall. He opens the flue of the fireplace and a mess of cinders and soot fall out, along with two dead bats and several stiff mice.

"Hey, Benno, should I try an' open this window," Moon calls, "an' get some of this dust to go out?"

"No!" Benno yells. "No, we wanna keep the front lookin' like it is . . . like no people is here."

"Why?" Juan asks. "Ain't no peoples out there. Wasn't no peoples all the way in to here."

"I say no, it's no," Benno says, giving Juan a stare. He isn't going to have some little kid ask him why he does what he does. He's the leader.

"Okay, okay," Juan replies.

Moon comes over. "I tol' ya. Don' ask too many questions."

"It's *one* question," Juan says, but Moon's look shuts him up.

After several hours, Benno's first promise comes true: The place looks so changed that it could not easily be recognized as the place they attacked with brooms and mops this very morning. They, themselves, are now sooty, dusty, filthy, and there is grit between their teeth as they sprawl on the floor or sit with their backs against the wall. It seems that all they can do is grin at one another. They grin so much that they start laughing, and they have no idea what they are laughing at. Suddenly Willie gets up and starts to do some slick breaks in the middle of the patterned floor. His back slides along the floor; he flips; he turns. Juan starts to whistle a tune for him and the others clap and laugh. And still nobody has anything real to say because they are overflowing with wordless feelings.

"Hey, I gotta get back an' help my ma wit the kids," Moon says, "an' Juan an' Paco gotta come wit me."

"Yeah, we all better be outta here fore . . . fore it gets real dark. But we kin come back tomorra."

They get ready to leave but Willie hangs back, kicking his blanket roll around instead of picking it up. "Listen," he says. "Listen, don't ya think we gotta have like a watchman here to take care of the . . . the prop'ty?"

"What d'ya mean?" Benno laughs. "Who been takin' care of it all this time it been a mess?"

"Tha's what I mean," Willie says, talking really fast and earnestly. "Now it ain't a mess no more. Now it . . . it's gonna be a great place fer, well . . . sleepin'. Some people might come an' grab it."

"Like who?" Juan asks. "Who knows, 'ceptin' us?"

Once again, Juan putting his nose in is annoying Benno, but there's something else bothering him, too.

"Wait," he says, looking closely at Willie. "Who'd ya think of fer this watchman, Willie?"

"I was sorta thinkin' of me," he says, slowly, ducking his face in embarrassment.

Benno exchanges glances with Moon. "What d'ya think, Moon?"

"Okay wit me," Moon says. "But there ain't nothin' to eat here."

Willie says, "I got some bread an' stuff in my pack. I kin get water in the cellar. I kin stay an' be a lookout guy fer ya."

"Ya not gonna be scared by yerself?" Paco asks.

"What of? Mice? I got rats big as bears in my alley."

"It's gonna be dark," Paco says.

"Dark!" Willie shrugs this off as one of the least important of matters. Darkness is not one of his fears. Attack by strangers is a fear; no place to sleep is a fear; freezing to death before morning is a fear; and loneliness, for as far as he can see, is a fear. And yet all these things lumped together, and more, are the facts of his life, and he is not afraid of life.

"Okay," Benno says, his heart beating very fast, but he does not stop to wonder why. "Okay, ya kin do it if ya wanna."

Willie grins and, without a moment's delay, unrolls his pack in front of the fireplace and sits down cross-legged.

"S'long Willie," Moon says. "We all gonna see ya tomorra."

"S'long," Willie says softly. "S'long."

They let themselves out through the basement window, but then Benno doesn't know what to do about the rubble he usually piles over that secret entrance. "We gotta leave it so he kin get out if he wants," he says. "Maybe I jus' pile the stuff up aroun' the edges, like." He does it; steps back to see the result; is satisfied; is, in fact, very elated, very high. He wants to stop and listen to the messages in his head, to think out what is happening and why he feels so terrific, but there isn't time. Through his preoccupation with closing the window, camouflaging it, and thinking about his feelings, he is conscious of the sound of dogs barking closer than usual. They'd better get out of here.

"Let's get outta here," Moon says, and this reinforces Benno's belief that Moon is plugged into his head. Now they retrace their steps, but this time Benno gives them instructions as they go, showing them the X's. "What I want," he says as they move swiftly, distancing themselves from the house, "I want us all to bring somethin' tomorra. Bring somethin' for cleanin'—rags, soap, mops, buckets, anythin' for cleanin'. Go aroun' the streets and bring anythin' you kin find. If ya use any cans in yer house for eatin' t'night, get them cans. We kin use 'em."

The sounds of dogs have been getting louder as they move away from the house. Moon is thinking this is strange and keeps looking over his shoulder. Now he sees them in the distance, running rhythmically in a pack, flying over the rubble. "Let's move it," he whispers to Benno: He doesn't want to scare the little kids. "Them wil' dogs is right down the street."

"Yeah," Benno says, picking up his pace, "I been hearin' 'em. Ya think they gonna come after us?"

"I dunno," Moon says, and now they are all nearly running, stumbling over the rubble. "I don' wanna know."

They are nearly at the borders of The Space when it becomes clear that the dogs are aware of them. They are in the same block with them, coming fast. Then suddenly they stop. They stand in a group, drawn back on their haunches, front legs stiff, ears laid back, barking angrily. The boys do not stand to watch them but reach the northern borders of the barrio and then run in earnest for the safety of the filthy, heavily populated, clamorous streets, protected by tenements full of known evils. Oddly, the dogs do not pass the borders of The Space. An invisible fence seems to hold them. They make parting growls and barks but turn and retreat.

Benno's heart is pounding, the little kids are out of breath; but now they can slow their pace.

"I ain't goin' back in there," Paco says. "Them dogs could eatcha."

"Naw," Moon says, though he, too, has had a real scare. "They jus' barkin' is all. We never even seen 'em before."

"One time is enough," Paco says. "I don' like that kinda dogs. And them dogs doesn't like us."

"Don' worry," Benno says, and he wonders if he means it. When they reach Benno's block he reminds them of the jobs he has assigned. "Remember to keep yer eyes open for anythin' we can use. We meet here tomorra, fronta my place here. Eight o'clock. Okay?"

"Okay," Moon and Juan say. Paco just looks at his feet encased in worn sneakers, covered with the grime of the day's work.

"Ya all done good," Benno says. "Real good." He just stands there and watches them go. These people have become very important to him, quickly. And more than that: He has become very important to them.

six

A child could float a paper boat in water flowing in the gutter of a crowded barrio, a teaming ghetto, and it would sail down the dirty street, pushing its way past garbage and turds, following the hydrant water down into the sewer. And if it were made of sturdy paper, it could float for hours under the city streets, dipping and turning deep down under the littered sidewalks and roadbeds until perhaps it might run aground under a cleaner street, under the handsomer house of a luckier child.

His boat can do that—escape the street—but can he?

*L*ast night Benno grabbed the cans that had contained the beans they had for supper, washed them out, and packed them into a plastic bag in which he was collecting things. He took a few rags from a bag his ma keeps for cleaning or mending. He scouted the tenement for little ends of soap and mushed them all together into a sizable cake. He has a stash of newspapers, which are the easiest thing to get out of the trash cans. The street people are not using so many of them in these mild spring months, whereas in winter they pack themselves in these newspapers for warmth, for bedding. He climbed into his sleeping bag, tired out from the day's activities, but had a hard time falling asleep. His mind was spinning. He kept seeing pictures of great spaces in perfect order, with rows of neat houses, and people nodding to each other, politely. Where could he have found such an image?

In the morning, Benno puts peanut butter on a couple of pieces of bread and puts them with a few carrots in his pack. He thinks maybe Willie doesn't have enough food for today. There is part of a cold sausage left from last night and he knows he could have had it for breakfast if he wanted, so he puts it in with the rest of the things.

Now he makes for the street, breathing through his mouth as he always does when he walks through the morning-smelling halls of the tenement. He walks along the streets like the old bag people, looking around the trash cans for anything at all. He finds a wire hanger, which he bends and puts in the bag. He grabs some more newspapers. When it feels like eight o'clock he is back at his building, just as Moon and the cousins round the corner. Nobody has a watch, but time works in them in some other way. They are loaded down with more old broken brooms and mops, which have been cleaned in the hydrant. Paco has a bottle of something sudsy he says he found in a laundromat. "It'll clean somethin'," he says.

"What d'ya mean, 'found'?" Benno asks, but he realizes the folly of this question. He will let Paco handle his own ethics right now. Later he will instill some moral principles in the citizens of Secret City. Just thinking that name brings a rush of good feelings to Benno: to Benno-the-Explorer, Benno-the-Pioneer, Benno-the-Founder of the Secret City—a place so secret that nobody speaks its name outside its boundaries. Later, oh later, they will do so many terrific things. For now, well, found is found.

Benno sees that Moon carries several dented galvanized pails and a couple of warped plastic ones. He also has a big sponge. "My Tio Chico give me the sponge," he says. "He got a couple to clean his cab, ya know. These buckets, people leave 'em fer a minute and some truck runs over 'em, but I'm straightenin' 'em out pretty good."

"Great!" Benno says. He jumps high in the air from pure good spirits, excitement, even happiness, which has not been with him since JoJo died. Once again, he has no time to look closely at his feelings. "Let's go," he says. "We got hard things to do today."

They pass a mission where, even at this early hour, thin and bedraggled people sit in chairs, singing a hymn, and looking at the table on which are arrayed paper cups and a coffee pot and a pile of donuts. The voices, hunger-full, float out over the morning air and into the awakening barrio. They have just passed a small old church on the corner when Benno gets an idea. "Wait up a minute," he says and, parking his plastic bag on the sidewalk, he pushes open the heavy door of the church and walks in. The air is chill compared to the outdoors and he shivers. He sees what he wants and, taking a little dull knife from his pocket, starts to scrape the melted wax from the glass votive lights. They ain't gonna do anything with these little ends, he thinks, are they?

He thinks that if he had time to ask, probably God, if he is around, would want him to have them. With this thought in mind, he stops scraping and "borrows" a few whole candles. "I'll return 'em sometime," he calls as he runs out and back to join the others.

The hike back to The Space is by the most direct route this time. Benno wonders when trust started: Did it start when they arrived with pails and mops? No, he doesn't think so. He wonders if it started when they all began to laugh last night.

When they cross into Poison territory, Benno has the others wait and he sneaks alone to the corner of a building that will give him a view of the last place he saw the gang. Nobody is there. He signals Moon. They're on their way again.

"Hey! We're here!" Paco says, as they enter the rubbled street on which the house stands. "But I don' know how we got here." He says this all with relief, because he has been hanging close to Moon and looking fearfully for dogs the whole time they've been in The Space.

Benno grabs a full bucket of water from under the pipe on the way upstairs, and puts another there in its place. "Ho! Willie!" he calls. There is the sound of feet upstairs and then the door at the top of the stairs is opened after a few tugs. Willie gives them a welcoming grin.

The kitchen looks different. There is a bucket under the sink. On one of the cupboard shelves they can see that Willie has put a plastic cup there, a dish, a spoon, a fork, and a knife. All the rest of Willie's things, whatever they might be, have been rolled neatly back into his bedroll.

"How'd it go, Willie?" Moon asks.

"Good," Willie says, smiling. "There ain't hardly a soun' 'cept fer the dogs. It ain't like the alley. No people is fallin' over ya. People ain't tryin' to pinch yer gear. Ya go to sleep and ya stay 'sleep all night. This here is a real good house we got."

"Whatcha doin' wit the pail?" Benno asks.

"Here, lemme show ya," Willie says. "This sink gonna be okay if we kin git a stopper fer it. See, ya jus' put water in it from another pail and wash somethin' or even yerself, and then ya pull out the stopper and the water goes into the pail. It kin go down the drain in the cellar if we kin fin' the right pipe an' some tools."

"Tha's good, Willie," Benno says. "Tha's real good."

Willie is trying very hard not to look too pleased. He swallows his smile by keeping his lips tight together and ducking his head.

Benno says, "Firs' thing, we gotta fix the crapper." And, while it would only take one of them, they all follow Benno upstairs, leaping over the steps with holes in them. They want to see what he's going to do.

"This room's what we gotta clean up, now," Benno says. "We ain't gonna have no grungy old sewer fer a bathroom like we got in our buildin's." He looks at the tub. "We kin even have a bath if we kin get 'nuf water up here." He goes over to the old toilet, reaches into the tank, and pulls out a few chunks of plaster and other flotsam. He jiggles the moving parts of the tank, takes the wire hanger he has brought, and twists off a piece which he attaches to the arm. Now he pours the contents of the bucket into the tank. There is no flushing lever, but Benno has not lived his life sharing tenement toilets for nothing. He knows how a toilet works. He reaches into the tank and lifts the rubber ball that stops the

61

drain. There is a strangled gurgle, a hiss, a splash, and water runs into the toilet bowl.

There is a cheer. "Tha's good, Benno," Moon says. "So now we jus' gotta keep puttin' water inna tank, right?" Moon has already started to give the bathroom the cleaning that Benno requested. The rest of them go down to start on other assignments.

Benno has so many plans it is hard for him to decide on which to do first. "Now, here the things we wanna do today or as soon as we kin." And he takes from his pocket a crumpled piece of torn paper and reads, "'See if toilet works': We done that. 'Clean more rooms. Get the junk outta the yard. Make a barricade.'"

"What kinda barricade?" Willie asks. "Where?"

"I'll show ya pretty soon," Benno says. "First, let's all go out an' work in that yard."

When they reach the yard, the howling of the dogs is loud and Paco stays close to the basement window, but the sound moves into the distance and he gradually inches toward the others. They have started to try to clear some of the yard of junk, throwing a lot of it into the next yard but saving anything worthwhile, stacking bricks, wires, pipes, et cetera, in piles around the edges of the area. From afar it looks like a kind of juggling act. Solid matter of all sizes is flying through the air: chunks of plaster, pieces of cement, indefinable objects of no known origin or use. And the piles along the edges begin to grow into a warehouse of useful things: pipes of all sizes, bolts, screws, nails, bent enamel pots, broken dishes and cups, pieces of dirty canvas, short lengths of lumber. When the sun is directly overhead, Benno surveys what they have done and calls a halt. "We gonna get somethin' to drink an' eat," he says.

At Benno's direction, they each bring up a cleaned can of water and set it in the sink. Benno puts one of his large cans into the sink and pours a little water into it. He washes his hands with a scrap of soap and then dumps the can and fills it again. "Nex'," he says.

When they have finished washing, Willie takes the bucket from under the sink and tosses the contents out the opened window. Benno thinks they will have to improve on that system once they get the yard really cleaned up. Maybe they can make a drain for the sink; but his mind is so full of other plans that he pushes that one back in line somewhere. They need more help.

"I din' bring much stuff to eat, but we kin share it," Benno says, as they arrange themselves in front of the empty fireplace. It turns out that everyone has brought something, and without another word, each offers part of his lunch to Willie, who has run out of food, just as Benno thought he would. Benno is wondering if anyone else notices that here, in The Space, in the house in Secret City, they are doing things they might never have done, probably, in their lives in the barrio: sharing the food is one of them; the tone of their voices is another— more sort of quiet, polite. They haven't had a fight since they have been here. There *is* something about The Space—that feeling he gets when he enters and loses when he leaves; the desire to do something important. And he feels the others must be touched by it, too, but he cannot ask them. It is somehow . . . embarrassing.

Willie is gobbling the piece of sausage like a hungry dog, and Benno, watching him, has another good feeling. He brushes at his eyes: He must have some dust in them.

Willie says, his mouth still full, "I was readin' some of

these here papers after you all leave me here, yestad'y. There's some weird stuff goin' on. I read how they put all the garbage in the city inna buncha big flat boats, all tied together, and they send those boats out'n the ocean to find someplace to put all this garbage 'cause there ain't no more room for garbage here. But they ain't 'llowed to dump it inna ocean neither, so they jus' boatin' round, boatin' round till they find somewheres to put it."

"Ya kin read the papers?" Benno asks.

"Yeah. Sometimes I don' have nothin' else to do. I don' read all the words, but I kin git the story pretty good."

"This is neat," Juan says, "like a picnic in the island we used to have."

But Benno has another image that he is grooving on: What they are doing is camping in the clearing of the wilderness. They are having their first meal in the new *land*. But as soon as he thinks that, he feels cut off and distant, more distant than he is ready to feel. So he re-thinks it. They are having their first meal in this new *city*—the Secret City—but not in a new land: "Secret City, U.S.A.," he says aloud.

"Whatdya say?" Willie asks.

Benno ducks his head. He had not realized till he heard his voice that he was thinking aloud. "Secret City, U.S.A.," he repeats more softly. "Tha's the real name of this place," he tells them.

"Yeah," Moon says, trying it on. "Tha's the name all right."

"Tha's the name ya dint tell us?" Paco asks.

"Yeah," Moon says, "an' ya don' say that name no-wheres but here. Hear me?" When he cautions the cousins, he does it in a soft voice. He does not yell at them unless they do something dangerous.

"I ain't gonna say it," Paco says.

"I like that name," Willie says. "It's . . . ya know . . ."

Everybody knows.

When it's time to go back to work, Juan is missing. They look around the rooms and then Willie sees him down in a corner of the newly cleared yard. He has a shovel without a handle and he is alternately digging and clawing at the packed soil.

"Hey, Juan!" Willie calls from the window. "Whatcha doin'?"

"Diggin'," Juan says.

"Yeah, I see ya diggin'," Willie says. "Whatcha diggin' fer?"

"Diggin' fer somethin' better'n a grave. Diggin' fer somethin' to grow."

"Great," Willie says, "jus' what we need—flowers. We need 'em firs' thing." He says it sourly.

"No, not flowers. Ya wait," Juan calls.

By the end of the day they have removed a great deal of debris from the house and swept it clean. A back window on each floor has been uncovered to allow light to filter in, and more or less cleaned on the inside. The bathroom is cleaner than any bathroom any of them has ever seen. They take turns sitting in the dry bathtub.

"How many buckets of water ya think it would take fer a real bath?" Willie asks.

"A lot," Benno says. "An' maybe ya wanna warm it, too."

"That ain't no good. Maybe we jus' sit in it an' throw a bucket over us."

"But the toilet works and it takes only one bucketful thrown into the tank."

Before they leave for the day, Willie volunteers to stay on as watchman again. And he has another request. "Say, Benno, when ya pass my alley and ya see a kid named Louie—real big, he is, looks older but he ain't. Tell 'im I'm gone a coupla days and he kin use my spot if he wants, but he gotta give it back when I want it. Okay?"

"Okay," Benno says. And then he asks, "What kinda kid's this Louie? I mean, he an okay kid? Like you?"

Willie is overwhelmed by the words, ". . . okay . . . like you," and Benno cannot believe that those words came out of his mouth. The fact that Willie has been nothing to him but a pesky little kid, until yesterday, *is* something he can understand, though—it's the "something" in The Space that changes people. He has come to accept that. Sometime he has to talk to Moon about that. He leaves Willie the candle scrapings and the two candles and a match book.

"Thanks," Willie says. "Tha's good." He settles on his bedroll, leans back, his knees up, his arms thrown wide, an enormous smile on his thin face.

"See ya, Willie," they call.

"See ya," Willie says.

It is late and dusk is falling when they scoot out from around the back of the house and into the rubbled street, preparing for the trek back. It is then that they see the unmistakable shape of a human darting in and out in the next block north. They fall back against their house and watch him. Has he seen them? Where is he going? Why? Is he a criminal? Is he dangerous? And in a moment he has disappeared. Disappeared, just like that!

They look at each other, none wanting to show fear. "Maybe," Benno says huskily, "maybe he jus' like us. Like he here 'cause he don' like it down where there so many people."

Yes, he is fearful, but more than that, he is upset that there is anyone else in The Space. He has no time to brood, however, because about a half block behind the darting figure, now disappeared, are two loudly barking dogs, running fast. Paco begins to whimper.

"They gonna eat us up," he wails.

"What ya, a baby?" Juan shakes him. "Ya ever know anyone what got et up by a dog?"

Benno knows they will have to take more steps to protect their holdings in The Space. "Tomorra," he says, as they hurry away, "we gonna build a stockade."

"Wha's a stockade?" Paco asks.

"Like what they build aroun' forts to protec' 'em from the Indians," Moon says. "But we can't get nearly all that wood," he says to Benno.

"Lemme worry 'bout that," Benno says. And he does: all night.

seven

*Dogs run wild in a dead City, where they
live by rules that are in their blood. Rats,
mice, pigeons, lice, fleas, roaches do not
leave. No, they stay on in relative peace.*

The mornings now have become a routine, and Benno
hopes that it is unnoticed in his neighborhood, where
a kind of hundred-character play is going on all day and
night, with enough else to interest anyone watching. But
he says, "Maybe we gotta go up there separate, sometimes, 'stead of allus goin' together. Maybe come back
separate, too. Them punks onna corner allus lookin' at
us goin' somewheres carryin' stuff. They gonna get wise
pretty soon, maybe."

Now he stops. They are at the alley, and sitting in
Willie's place against the wall is a kid who was once in
their class but got thrown out. Benno slaps his own forehead. "I fergot to do what Willie tol' me to do 'bout his
spot."

"Hey!" he challenges the kid in the alley. "Whatcha
doin' there? Ain't that Willie's spot?"

"Yeah," the boy says defensively. "An' I'm keepin' it fer 'im. Willie, he's gone 'way right now."

"Oh yeah? Where he's gone?" Benno asks, innocently but sarcastically.

"Uh . . . well . . . he jus' 'way, like."

"Where ya been hangin' out fore ya took Willie's spot?"

"Who wants to know?" says the boy, but not very energetically.

Benno, now surly—he has his reputation as leader to uphold, a heavy responsibility—says, "Me, tha's who," and he pulls himself up into a tall and belligerent stance, even though he knows that, standing up, this kid is surely bigger than he is.

The boy seems too lazy to rise to the bait. He waves his arm idly and answers Benno's question. "I hang out jus' back there," he says, and Benno can see, in the shadowed alley, unclear figures of people and trash cans merged into strange shapes. An idea grows on him slowly.

"Yer name Louie?" he asks.

"Yeah. How d'ya know that?"

"Ya hung out here a long time?" Moon asks.

"Jus' since . . . since spring. Since my ma got took to the hospital. Why ya askin' all them questions?"

"Whatsamatter wit yer ma?" Benno asks.

"Aw . . . we got put outta the place where the city put us and she got somethin' in her ches' while we was livin' inna street."

"Was ya in one of them welfare hotels?" Juan asks.

"Yeah, we was in lots of 'em."

"I know," Juan says. "We was, too. My brother— tha's him—and me, and my mother and her new kid." He shudders, remembering.

"Street's better'n them," Louie says. "But I get kick outta school 'cause I keep movin' alla time. I don' mind. Me, I ain't no good in school, but I don' want my li'l brother to grow into no bum like me."

"Where ya kid brother at?" Benno asks, and Louie points to a child about Paco's age, curled in a ball, fast asleep nearby.

"I in charge of 'im now my mama ain't here. We gotta keep movin' movin' so nobody take 'im 'way from me."

Benno wants to talk this over with Moon. He puts his packages down between his feet and raises his hands and slowly moves his hands in the sign language Moon has taught him. "This an okay kid?" he signs.

Moon replies slowly so that Benno can read, "I saw him around, and I never saw him with punks. I never saw him drunk or dealing, but that doesn't mean he doesn't."

Benno turns back to Louie, who has now begun to gather his stuff and is reaching over to awaken his brother. "How ya gonna keep the kid from bein' a bum if ya keep 'im onna street?"

Louie looks troubled for a minute, but then he says, "Oh, we ain't allus gonna be onna street. We got plans."

"What kinda plans?" Benno asks.

"Well . . . Why you askin' all this?"

"Ya don' wanna tell me, don'." Benno turns around, and Louie continues with only a moment's hesitation.

"When my ma be all right, we all gonna move to the country inta a reg'la' house, wit a door, wit a garden . . ."

"I'm makin' a garden," Juan says.

"Hey, Louie," Benno says. "How'd ya like to come 'long wit us?"

70

"Yeah? Where?" Louie is properly suspicious. Nobody takes offense. In this block . . . in this city . . . in this world, they have all learned not to expect offers without looking for the catch in them. Benno thinks that suspicion is something with a shape. It comes and stands between you and someone. It is not a sharp shape, like being mad: It is a sort of spongy thing with a gray color. He sees Louie's suspicion form up between them. Louie's response is sort of sullen, not hopeful as Willie's has been.

"We goin' somewheres secret. Ya wanna go, ya gotta trus' us . . . an' we gotta trus' ya."

"Oh yeah?" Louie says. The suspicion is still there, but it is weakened now by interest. "How come?"

"Yeah, ya right," Benno says. "Okay. Ya ever been tangled wit a gang?"

"No real tangle, like, but I used to work fer 'em in a other place I lived."

"Ya ain't tangled now?"

"No, I ain't."

"Ya ever be in trouble like wit the p'lice?"

"Sure I have," and Louie's reply tastes of pride.

"Whatdya do?"

"Oh, I done a few things. Like I say, I run errands fer this buncha punks. Then I run errands fer a pusher an' they got 'im, an' *I* ain't goin' where they put 'im, so I ain't doin' it no more. An' I ain't doin' it fer *no body* else neither."

"We ain't pushin' nothin'," Benno says. "I'll tell ya, we goin' where Willie is, right now."

"Yeah?" Louie's face relaxes. "All *right!*" he says. "Willie wit ya, I am, too. This here is Ozzie," he says, pulling the little ragbag of a child out of his ragbag bed.

71

"We're goin', Ozzie," he says. "Git yer stuff." And Ozzie bundles up his rags and makes a quick dive into the dumpster, coming up with a can, partly filled with Pepsi, and a hunk of something that might have been a pizza.

"Okay then," Benno says, looking at the new recruits. "Le's go."

"I don' like this here territory," is the only thing Louie says to them as he follows them uptown and into the murky area, woven with alleys, where the Poisons hang out. No one asks him why and Moon is the one who scouts the area before they turn corners. They have all followed him around the last corner except Louie and Ozzie when they hear sounds coming from the street they have just left.

"I thought that was you, Louie," a gravelly voice is saying. "Where ya been, huh?"

They all freeze. Then Benno inches back to the corner on his stomach and peers around the corner. There's Louie, all right, and there's a very sharp looking, brightly dressed punk, his head shaved, standing with his hand on Louie's shoulder, drawing him backward, unbalancing him, so he falls to the sidewalk. Ozzie is standing with his hands over his eyes.

"Ya still owe Big George, Louie, and ya know 'im: He don' carry credit this long, ya hear. He's gonna be in touch." And he twists Louie's ear before he disappears into the alley. Slowly, Louie picks himself up, and, holding Ozzie's hand, he joins the others. He looks stricken.

"What ya tol' us ain't the truth!" Benno charges. "Yer wit a gang, the Poison gang!"

"No I ain't and I weren't," Louie says. "But I ran fer them; I done errands, like I tol' ya."

"So why's this creep leanin' on ya?" Benno asks.

"'Cause they still want me to work fer 'em. I owe 'em fer . . . fer . . . fer somethin' they give me. But I can't pay 'cause I ain't got no money, so they say I gotta work it out. But I don' wanna do that stuff no more."

"We gonna b'lieve 'im?" Benno asks Moon.

"I guess we gotta," Moon says. "Why he be hangin' out in our alley, if'n he still workin' fer 'em?"

"I hidin' out from 'em," Louie says. "I figure they forget me."

"Yeah, I guess," Benno says, and they resume the trek. He wants it to be true, but he doesn't feel entirely sure.

So it is that six people arrive at The Space—the roundabout way, until they can be sure of Louie.

"Oh wow!" Louie says. "This here is like a disaster place. This is like a war. I hear 'bout this place. What d'ya wanna do up here? There's wild dogs up here." Paco runs behind Juan and holds on to the end of his shirt.

"Yeah?" Benno pretends surprise. "Who tol' ya?" He's worried. Who of this band might talk? He can't really imagine. Maybe Moon's squeaky little cousin.

"Some big toughs I used to know. They knew some guys used to live here. But don' nobody come here now."

"*We're* here," Paco says.

At their house, they find that Willie is already at work. He is hauling a big piece of rubble to the end of the street. He has started a wall.

"Hey! Tha's jus' what I was plannin' fer us to do today," Benno says. "Ya read my mind, Willie."

"Ho, Willie!" Louie calls.

"Ho, *Louie*!" cries Willie when he sees this oversized boy. "Hey, Benno, ya brung 'im 'long! Whatcha thinka this place, huh?" he asks Louie. "Ho, Ozzie," he adds.

"I dunno what I think," Louie says. "I never seen nothin' so mess up in my life."

"Yeah ya have," Benno says. "Ya seen the block where we live at, where ya was yer own self. It mess up in a differnt way . . . like wit people; like wit people doin' rotten stuff. This place, it jus' mess up wit the kinda junk we kin git ridda it." He gives Willie a newspaper package of some food he's scrounged from last night's supper, and Willie stops his work and gobbles it down. Willie has no pattern of eating at regular hours or particular foods suitable for morning, noon, or night. His stomach has no expectations of such luxury. It accepts whatever he pushes its way, whenever he can. It tries to convert this irregular fuel to enough energy to provide Willie with the strength to withstand what he must.

"Yer never gonna get ridda this stuff," Louie says scornfully. "Ya need a hunderd people an' a steam shovel to do that."

"Yeah!" Juan says. "Well, ya wanna see what we already done, then. Kin I show 'im, Benno?"

"Yeah," Benno says. "Show 'im." He is worried again. Have they a dissenter here, a negative voice? Did he make a mistake? Is this kid trouble?

"Hey, Willie," Moon says, when Juan has led Louie around the side to the entrance of the house. "This guy Louie, he a frienda yers, right?"

"Yeah, right," Willie replies. "He's okay. Don' worry. He so big, see, he allus havin' t'take on the big punks. He allus suspicious 'bout anythin' diff'rent. He gotta be: He ain't lucky."

Benno nods. He will have to be content with Willie's street-wise estimate and keep his eyes open. Now they all pitch in to start clearing the street. Louie is right: It looks like an endless task, like emptying a river. But, taking one little section at a time, they begin to see that they are accomplishing two things: They are clearing up the street in front of the house and, by piling the rubble at the ends of the street, they are building a barricade— Benno's stockade.

"If we make it wide at the bottom," Moon says, studying the engineering possibilities, "it won' tip over, like."

"Yeah, but won' it slide down?" Benno says.

"Some will, some won'," Moon says. "Tha's what I think."

Louie has returned from his tour and he is silent. Nobody asks him anything. He stands around watching for a few minutes and then he starts lugging enormous pieces of masonry. If a piece is too big to carry, he rolls it over and over until it is at the base of the barricade.

"Geez!" Moon exclaims, surprised and frankly admiring. "I din' think we could move that kinda stuff, not at all. I already tried wit Willie." Louie doesn't say anything, but he looks pleased.

Once again the sun tells them it is lunchtime. They sit down on a cleared spot in the street and take things from their pockets and pool them.

"Hey," Willie says. "I fergot to tell ya. Ya kin drink the water in the house."

"Yeah? How ya know that?" Benno asks. It is one of the things he has been worrying about: where to find potable water.

"Easy," Willie says. "I tried it an' I'm still here. One thing I know 'bout is what ya kin eat and what ya can't eat."

Benno thinks about this piece of good news. He is inclined to trust Willie's judgment of the water supply.

Who, after all, would be better able to judge than a boy who has been choosing his own food and drink from the garbage of the city for long enough to know he can stay alive? Like animals know what's okay for them to eat, Benno thinks.

"Okay," he says. "Willie, you be in charge of the water supply 'cause you the person stayin' here. Keep collectin' it in cans—we brang a lot more—till we kin figger out somethin' else."

"So this where yer stayin', eh, Willie?" Louie says. "This place sure is better'n our alley, hey? I never seen no house like that. I keepin' yer place fer ya though, fer when ya get sicka bein' here."

Benno and Moon exchange a question and answer, with a kind of eye and head signal, and as usual, Moon signs his answer with his hands.

"Hey, Louie," Benno asks, "maybe you an' yer brother like to stay here fer a while, too?" He tries to act casual, as if this is of no particular importance to him one way or another.

Louie takes his time answering. "Well, I dunno. I got this good place inna alley, while Willie he ain't there. Don' wanna lose that place."

"Whatever ya say," Benno says, starting to roll a big piece of concrete over and over until it leans on the barricade.

"Well, I gonna think on it," Louie says. "We gotta even this barricade off," he says, squinting at the effect of the the wall. "I think I gonna hold out all these here bricks to put outside the pile, see. Make it look more like a real wall."

"Tha's a good idea, Louie," Moon says. "Benno, if he gonna stay, maybe we make Louie in charge buildin'

76

the wall on 'count of he's strong and he got these ideas 'bout it."

"Okay, Louie, ya wanna be in charge?" Benno asks.

Louie doesn't know how to take this. Here are a bunch of kids he never talked to except in passing. Never knew their names. First they ask him to come with them; then they ask him to stay here; now they ask him to be in charge. Something is fishy. Nobody ever asked him to stay anywhere. Nobody ever asked him to be in charge of anything. Because he is so big, people are always expecting he is going to act some way he can't. Now, here are all these kids . . .

"I gonna think on it," he says again. After a while, without saying anything, he starts rolling debris toward the other end of the block to start the other barricade. Benno and Moon exchange looks again. They think Louie is on board.

When Benno and Moon are together on one side of the street, Willie comes over to them. "I tol' ya 'bout the water," he says. "That there is the good news. I gotta tell ya somethin' else. I seen somebody."

"Yeah," Benno says. "We seen somebody, too. When ya see 'im?"

"I thought I seen somebody yestad'y in the mornin', but I wasn't sure. I thought maybe it's a dog. I din' see 'im clear. But las' night I see 'im pretty good from the back window. What we gonna do?"

"I guess we not gonna do nothin' yet," Benno says. "We gotta see who he is an' see where he live. We gotta keep our eyes open. If he live here, he gotta know we got this house. We ain't been quiet. An' anyways he ain't done nothin'. Maybe it ain't bad."

"Maybe," Willie says without conviction, but without

fear. Benno thinks that this scrawny kid is really a very brave kid.

Paco has been working with Louie's little brother, Ozzie, and Ozzie is helping Paco sort out smaller junk in the road. It seems that Ozzie will talk to Paco, but to nobody bigger than he is except Louie. Benno surveys the scene. Seven of us, he thinks, all working here, cleaning this up, making something terrific. Because now that Louie and Ozzie have joined them, he knows what all of them are doing. It has come clear in his head, in a way that he can fully understand it, and the enormous feeling that overwhelms him, as he comes to see every-thing clearly, would have sent him tearing up the stairs to the roof back in the tenement. But here he just picks up the biggest piece of broken cement he can lift to his shoulder and carries it down the street and puts it on the top of a section of wall. There it remains—a monument to the moment.

When it is time to leave, Juan says, "Me an' Paco, we wanna stay a little longer today. Okay?"

Moon says, "Yer ma gonna kill me if ya ain't home when she wants ya."

"A hour only," Juan says. "Willie, Louie, an' Ozzie, they here, too. Maybe they walk part way back wit us. It stay light pretty long now."

"Listen," Moon says. "Ya ain't babies. Ya gotta learn to take care yerselfs, but ya be careful, hear. Keep watchin' fer trail marks we showed ya."

"Le's go, then," Benno says, and he and Moon start the trek out of the wilderness.

"Maybe I shouldn't of oughta left 'em," Moon says.

"I'm s'prised Paco wanna stay."

"No dog et 'im yet," Moon says.

78

How much tidier their street is now. They notice this as they make their way back through the tumbled-down wasteland. Benno is just saying this to Moon when their ears are assaulted by a hideous growling. Without a word, they jump into a tiny rubbled alley between two partly wrecked buildings, stumbling over the debris as they do it. Now, from around the corner, two enormous dogs charge, tearing at each other's throats, followed by a pack of six dogs, barking and yelping, almost seeming to be cheering the two combatants on. Both fighters are bloody and it appears that they will kill each other.

Benno and Moon do not dare to move; they barely dare to breathe. They watch with horrified fascination as the dogs force each other backward and forward, slowly moving the arena farther down the street, but their snarling gets weaker as blood flows from their wounds. Then, with a frightening leap, one of the dogs grabs the throat of the other and shakes it. There is silence for a moment and then the winner lets go. All the other dogs move in now and begin to pull at the dead dog. Benno feels like vomiting.

"Oh, jeez!" he says. "If somebody tol' me that . . . You gonna b'lieve that, Moon, somebody tol' ya somethin' like that? I never seen nothin' like that."

"No," Moon says. "I seen toughs fightin' wit knives but I never seen nobody bein' et. Oh, jeez!" he exclaims. "I gotta go back fer the li'l kids now."

"Yeah," Benno says. "Paco gonna be scared to death. I'll go wit ya. Ya think we kin git outa here now?"

"They so busy eatin', maybe they won' notice us," Moon says. "I *hope!*"

Staying very low and close to the building, they move around the corner and out of sight of the slavering dogs.

It is not their regular route, but they dare not follow the signs now. Slowly they weave their way back, keeping an eye out for the dogs, making mistakes, but finally ending up at the street behind the house.

"Maybe sometime we clear a path to this back way in," Benno says, relieved to be on home turf.

They find Juan and Paco in the yard, cowering under the steps.

"Whatcha doin' there?" Moon asks.

"We dint know it was you makin' all the noise in the backyards. We think it maybe somebody . . ."

"Like who else?"

"Well, ya know, we seen someone yestad'y."

"Well, it ain't nobody else," Moon says. "We come back fer ya 'cause . . . well, it gonna be better that way."

"Hey, whatcha doin' in the yard?" Moon asks, now, as he sees a little square of ground has been dug deep and loose.

"Ah, this is a s'prise," Juan says.

"A garden," Paco says. "A garden fer veg'ables."

"Yer kiddin'," Benno says.

"No," Paco protests. "Inna island, we got a garden. We know how. Here, there was a garden before."

"See how black the earth is," Juan says. "That kinda ground's good for growin'. We see li'l sprouts and we think things are growin' here already. An' we plant squash."

"Where'd ya git 'em?" Benno asks, forgetting his advice to himself about asking people where they got things.

"We save 'em," Paco says.

"Tha's true," Moon says. "They save all kinda seeds

80

when my ma cooks, and then they dry 'em. Then they roast 'em and eat 'em sometimes, like nuts."

"Only now we plant 'em instead of roast 'em," Juan says.

"We gonna plant other things, too," Paco says. "Sprouts, they grow quick, like in a coupla days."

"Wow!" Benno says. "Okay, kids, you got a special job. Terrific!"

"Yeah, it's terrific, all right," Moon says. "But we gotta get home now."

"Nah," Juan says. "We got a lot more we wanna do."

"Tomorra," Moon says. "Move it."

The light is beginning to fail, and they hurry through the darkening wasteland and arrive in their old world just as dusk is falling. The streetlights go on and illuminate the message-marked walls—red, blue, black, yellow, words and names in luminous paint. Against the walls lean old men, old women, families, preparing themselves for another night on the street.

Benno regards them with the same discomfort and embarrassment that he always has. But right now he is so relieved to have avoided the dogs, that is his strongest feeling. But that's the way it is to be in the wilderness, he thinks. It could have been wolves or bears. Sure, he was a little frightened. Once, years ago, he told JoJo that he had been scared by something in the street and JoJo said, "Good. It's smart to be scared if there is something to be scared of. Then you will be careful and you will learn." He had felt better then about being scared. He bets Moon was scared this time, too. He hopes so.

eight

Today, yesterday, tomorrow: In a dead City they do not mean anything. There is no time: It is suspended. Something new is created that fills the space that time once did. Is it promise?

*D*espite all the time spent in The Space and his strong interest in what they are doing, Benno sometimes feels strangely discontented. He finds himself standing still, leaning on the broom handle, staring out over the desolate landscape. He sometimes snaps at Juan or at Willie when they interrupt these meditations. But he doesn't know what is bothering him. It's something that hits him as they walk into The Space now. There is still that overwhelming good feeling, but underneath that is this other bad feeling. And then the bad feeling hits him again when he leaves The Space, working its way into his head like a piece of a puzzle, squirming and twisting to fit just the right place. It's something that makes him feel down when he thinks he should be feeling up.

Like yesterday, when they were on their way to The Space very early in the morning. The streets looked deceptively clean because it had rained all night. In the alleys and in many doorways, street people were unwrapping themselves from soggy blankets, cardboard, or newspapers; emerging as the contents of large cartons; shaking themselves like wet dogs; mumbling to each other and to themselves. One woman was unwinding each of her children from sheets of plastic as if they were packages, examining them to see if they were damaged in shipping. One of the little children was crying, but the woman seemed so troubled herself that she was unable to do anything for him.

"Do Not Litter" read a sign on a pole near the spot where the family had been encamped. "Fine or Imprisonment or Both." The pole itself was surrounded by black, green, and brown plastic bags of garbage, their sides ripped, their contents spilling onto the pavement to join the other fly-ridden, unidentifiable muck that settled there. Benno took in this scene in with the bad feeling rising. They're like the garbage, he had thought. They're dumped onto the street like the garbage.

When he ran to join the others, who had stopped to wait for him a block away, Moon asked, "Where ya been?" "Where have I been?" Benno had asked himself. "I've been right where I am alla time, only now . . . only now it looks diff'rent." For reasons he does not understand, his eyes seemed to have been turned on. Instead of trying to run from the sights and smells of his neighborhood or dream them away, he was seeing them, *really seeing them,* as if for the first time, with more than just his eyes, and it was making him feel sick and, somehow, different.

"Where ya been," Moon asked again, as they resumed their trek to The Space.

"Nowheres," Benno replied.

And again today he stops for a moment to watch the morning life of the street. There is yet another mother with three little children, sitting atop a fire hydrant, surrounded by bundles, trying to get one of the children to help carry a few. She herself has to carry the youngest child, as well.

"It's too heavy, Ma," complains the oldest child, trying to balance a package bigger than he is.

"Take this here one, then," the woman says. "Come on! Pick it up. Ya *gotta*! There ain't no other way. We gotta get to the shelter, else all the space gonna be gone again."

"Where's it at, Ma?" the oldest child asks.

"Near here, somewheres."

"Is it somewheres we stayed before? Huh?"

"I dunno. I don' 'member 'em all."

"I gonna have a cot fer myself?"

The mother snorts. "Ya kiddin'? Alla ya shut up, now, and come on." And, trailing bits of plastic bags, dragging their bundles along the filthy streets—eyes large, turning to watch a man who is munching on a roll—this little caravan in the concrete desert files to its next oasis with the hope that it will not have dried up before they arrive.

Benno has fallen behind Moon and the little kids while he's been watching the street scene. Why? he asks himself, as he hurries to catch up. Why am I feeling so rotten? Why today? This is no different from the many times he has witnessed such scenes. These people, and people like these, are part of what he knows, what he sees daily and hates—the squashing of people in the city until they overflow the spaces they are in, till they join the refuse in the street.

They're nearing The Space, Benno still deep in his thoughts, making all the turns by habit, when he feels a hand on his shoulder and a scratchy voice says, "Hold it, right there!" They freeze. "Hold it, ya buncha li'l nuttin's." The face belonging to the voice now appears in front of them. It's the same punk with the POISON T-shirt who had stopped Louie and yelled at them before. "Who ya think ya lookin' at?" the scratchy voice charges, the face coming in close.

"Ain't lookin' at nobody," Benno says, remembering the knife honed to a curve.

"Well, I think ya lookin' at me 'cause it's me is right in fronta ya. Ya wanna know somethin'?"

They all nod. A nod is what is asked for, surely.

"I think it be real queer that the same nuttin' kids is standin' aroun' lookin' at us when they was doin' the same thing before. Plus, here is a coupla other nuttin's. So I think maybe somethin' goin' on. Tha's what I think."

"It jus', like, happens," Moon says. "See, this is on the way to where we go to spen' the day wit . . . wit my uncle. He sick."

Benno is surprised. This is the first time he has heard Moon lie so glibly. It takes his mind off the immediate trouble.

"Uncle, huh? Live where?" Moon waves in the general direction of north. "Ain't nothin' up there 'cept wild dogs an' rats. This uncle, he a wild dog or he a rat?" This breaks up the Poison guy, and he is joined in his laughter

85

by a few other Poisons who have appeared from nowhere. But they sober up and the tough takes his sharp knife and cuts a curved mark right across the sneaker of each kid. They hold their breath; they don't believe it. "See that! See how sharp. I prob'ly dint even cut yer feet much. Tha's dainty. Tha's a dainty knife. It cut anythin' I want. Now next time, I gonna tell it to cut right through." Paco is crying now. "Why ya wanna drag a li'l kid 'long fer? Some spies! Some rats! Ya tell yer He-Devil gang to look sharp. Better sen' diff'rent spies. We is on to these ones." And he ambles away, loose limbed.

Benno is just as scared as he knows the others are, but he says, "The guy's stoned outta his head." They speed out of there and it is with relief that they reach the good bright air of The Space.

The encounter with the Poison gang has distracted Benno from his thoughts, but he still wants to talk to Moon about what has been going through his mind during the last few days, now that his heart has stopped pounding. When everyone is working away at the usual daily tasks, Benno collars Moon.

"Here's what I been thinkin'," he says, knowing he will have a willing ear. "Here we got this whole Space. It belongs to us." When Moon starts to interrupt, Benno shuts him up and goes right along with this thought before he loses it somewhere in the rubble. "We got this whole 'normous Space to ourself." His face gets tense and urgent. "Moon, we gotta get some of them street people up here and give 'em somewheres to stay, somewheres that could be like their own—just like we done— somewheres nobody gonna rob 'em, kick 'em aroun', mug 'em, move 'em from one rotten place to another rotten place. Moon, we *gotta do somethin'*."

Moon looks at his friend closely. "How we gonna do that? Whatcha gonna do—go 'long the street wit a sign says 'foller me'? Benno, they so many! And some of 'em is sick . . . very bad sick. Some of 'em is funny in their heads. Some of 'em is crackheads an' worse. A lot of them people needs to be inna hospital. My Tio Chico tell me that. How ya gonna tell if they okay?"

"How we know 'bout Willie an' Louie an' Ozzie?" Benno says.

"We jus' went wit what we was feelin' 'bout them."

"Then tha's how we do it. Look how good that work out. Louie, Willie, Ozzie, they not sick in the head, they jus' got bad luck. Louie, his ma sick. Willie, I think his pa in jail. Lookit that lady and them three kids we see jus' this mornin'. Ya think she don' want somewheres to put all that junk down and somewheres the kids could go to sleep the same place ev'y night, outta the rain?"

Moon nods his head in understanding. "Yeah, ya right. It jus' a big, big job."

"But tha's it. This is a big big space. *Somebody* gotta do somethin' 'bout it, and we the only people here to do it. How many people ya think there is like that out there?"

Moon says, "I dunno. Prob'ly hunderds or t'ousands."

"We gotta think on it," Benno says. "Ya know how them Poisons own all that turf down there? They kin do anythin' they want." He almost shouts that in frustration. "An' everythin' they want is no good. So how come, if we got a turf fer ourself up here, how come we can't do somethin' good?"

"Yeah," Moon says. "We gotta think on it."

Benno calls a halt to work a little early.

"Now we gonna have a meetin'," he says. "I'm gonna

be president of the meetin' an' what I wanna know is if ya know other kids, like personal, or even maybe some bigger people, who stay inna streets."

"Ya kiddin'," Louie hoots. "'Ceptin' you an' Moon an' them little kids, most alla folks I know lives inna street."

"Sure, I know a bunch of 'em, too. Why ya wanna know?" Willie says.

"'Cause what we gotta do—we gotta git lotsa people, they need a place to stay, an' get 'em up here in The Space an' give 'em all a place to stay at." Benno speaks rapidly and with great anxiety. "We gotta get 'em up here and start 'em fixin' more houses. Then they prob'ly know more people and they know more . . . and like that."

"Hol' on," Willie says. "How come, when I come wit ya, ya ask me all them questions—am I okay an' all like that? Now, ya gonna git all them people, how ya gonna know they okay?"

"Yeah, Benno, whatcha gonna do if they winos, an' druggies, or punks wit knives?" Moon asks. "What gonna happen to the Secret City then?"

"Yeah," Louie says. "Like one of 'em get picked up by the cops and he tell 'em where we all at. Good-bye secret!"

"I don' think so," Benno says.

"Why?" Moon asks.

Benno walks around a bit: He is actually embarrassed to put into words what he wants to say, but he's got to try.

"Ain't no one noticed it but me?" he begins. "Ain't ya noticed how people is kinda diff'rent in here?"

"What people?" Willie asks.

88

"Us people," Benno says.

"Diff'rent how?" Moon asks.

"Well, ya know, sorta not so . . . not so sorta . . . well, mean, like." Now the rest comes in a rush. "I think somethin' goin' on about The Space that maybe take the bad outta people. Lookit, we ain't had a fight since we been here. Right?"

"Yeah, right," Moon says. "But you and me don' fight much anyways."

"You and me, maybe; but I fight wit other people, or I cuss 'em out, an' I fight wit my ma and pa . . . like wit words. Lookit how we doin' all this stuff fer each other, not jus fer ourself, like." He's through, red as a beet and looking at the floor.

Louie looks at the sky and whistles, but Willie says, "Well, maybe, but maybe that don' work on ev'ybody."

Moon sighs. He puts up with a lot with this friend; he is a patient person, Moon is. "My Tio Chico, he got a couple guys sleep in his cab some nights," he says. "If they was real no-goods, he wouldn' let 'em."

Benno is relieved: They have not laughed him down. "Well then, when ya see 'em, ya talk to 'em. Okay?"

"A other kid stay in our alley lotsa times," Willie says. "He from Haiti and talk kinda funny and he just a kid, too. I don' think he into anythin' bad. He got some kinda voodoo tell him don' do nothin' bad. I seen 'im wit it. Maybe some punks ask 'im, 'Ho, Alf, ya run a li'l job fer us?' Alf, he take his voodoo gizmo an' he swing it aroun'. It say yes, he do it; it say no, he don' do it. I think the gizmo work pretty good."

"Ya wanna talk to 'im, see if he wanna come 'long?" Benno asks.

"Yeah," Willie says. "I meet ya at the alley in the mornin'. Maybe he be there then."

Willie keeps his appointment, and in the morning when Benno, Moon, Juan, and Paco appear, he is already in conversation with a small, dark boy with enormous eyes that are fixed on Willie.

"Whatcha mean 'leev een houz? Ain't no people gonna geev me room een real houz. Why you theenk I sleep here!"

"Listen, Alfie," Willie says. "I unnerstan' ya 'cause I stay in this here alley longer even 'n you. Right?"

"Dot's right," Alf agrees. "An' now I got dat spot," and he chuckles.

"Yeah, and yer gonna give it back if I come back," Willie says. "But maybe . . . not sure, but maybe I ain't comin' back on 'ccount of I got this neat place to stay an' I givin' ya a invite to come stay there an' help fix it."

Now Willie spies the others, as they enter the alley cautiously. "See, here's my friends now. This here is Alfonzo 'n' this here is Benno, Moon, Juan, 'n' Paco."

"Ho!" Benno says, as the others grunt greetings.

"He not sure he wanna come," Willie says.

"If he don' wanna," Benno says, "we don' want 'im."

"Well, whatcha say, Alf?" Willie asks. "We gotta get goin'. Ya comin'?"

Alf removes from his pocket a strange object that looks like a yellowed piece of smooth wood. It is irregular in shape and hangs from a dark blood-red old string. He squats and holds it still for a moment, whispering a few words, then he lets it hang freely from his fingers. First it just seems to hang still, but slowly it begins to sway back and forth, side to side, side to side, back and forth. "Ees okay," Alf says brightly. "I go wif you." And he gathers up his things.

The others exchange glances and shrugs, palms turned up and raised. "What's happening?" one gesture asks. "Don't know," the other gesture replies, in a sign language that everybody knows.

With Benno in the lead, the safari begins, Paco bringing up the rear, running fast to keep up with the strides of the bigger kids. He has ceased complaining about the dogs.

As they move farther from the familiar neighborhood, Alf lets out little exclamations of amazement. "Hey! Where ees all de people?" he asks, when they have entered the streets that are almost empty. "Where dey gone?" And, "Hey!" he says soon after that, "look at all dees stuff een de street. How a car drive een here?" But when they arrive at the border of The Space, he stops cold.

"No, mon, no! I don' go eento no place like dees place. You listen? You hear? You put out your han', you feel? Dees place ees for bad. You see." And again, he takes from his pocket the little charm with the strange markings, and holds it in his dusty dark fingers, dangling it from its red string that looks as if it had been dyed in blood.

"Hey!" Benno has had it with this seeming nonsense. "What *is* that?"

"True bone," Alf says softly, his big eyes round and serious. "Eet tell de truf. Hush now." He squats and draws a circle in the dust and divides it into four sections and in each section he draws a mark. Now he dangles the true bone over the circle and watches as it moves around, slowly swinging over one square and then over another and finally coming to rest.

"See!" Alf says. "True bone say eet no good."

"How'd it say that?" Benno challenges. "Jus' how'd it say that? I din' hear it say nothin'." The others titter nervously.

Alf looks at them pleasantly. He has not taken offense at their doubts. Perhaps he has heard them before from others. "Ya jus' gotta know, mon," he says. "Ya gotta know how to leesten, how to watch. I got no time fer teach ya. Ya jus' gotta trus' me." And he smiles a nice open smile. But now, as he watches, the charm starts to move again. "Jus' a meenute! Jus' a meenute! Eet move some more. What eet say? Eet say yes; eet say no." He looks closely at the charm, challenging it. "Whatcha say?" And the true bone starts moving around in a circular path, picking up speed, until it is whirling. Alf looks panicked. "Eet never do dot before today," he says, his face contorted as if he were in pain. His faith is being shaken loose. Is the true bone failing him after all these years? He sits quietly, looking into the distance, trying to find the answer, which has always been given him by the true bone.

Benno, who has been restlessly waiting for the seance to end, gets an idea. "Hey!" he says. "Maybe it tellin' ya that part of The Space is okay and part of it ain't." And Moon, who has been measuring the distance of the dogs by the volume of their barks and howls, nods his head vigorously.

Alf looks at Benno with hope in his eyes. Then he addresses the true bone. "Ees dot eet?" he asks. And, as he holds the string, the bone starts slowly to move back and forth, back and forth. "Eet say yes," Alf says, brightening. "Come on, I go wif ya."

"How ya like that!" Benno whispers to Moon. "Ya think there anythin' to this here true bone?"

"How do I know?" Moon answers. "It tol' him true, all right."

And so now they are eight strong—the citizens of Secret City—and growing, thinks Benno. Inside him a voice is calling out "JoJo! Ya see me? Ya see what we doin'?" And he yearns to ask Alf to see if the true bone can tell the answer, but he cannot.

They arrive at the house to find a pile of sticks which have sharp points at one end piled in a corner of the kitchen.

"Wha's this stuff?" Benno asks.

"They jus' sticks," Louie says. "Ho, Alf!" he says heartily.

"Ho, Louie," Alf says.

"What we need them sticks fer?" Moon asks Louie.

"Aw, I don' know. I jus' think ya might wan' 'em."

"Yeah," Juan says. "They good fer when the beans is up. We let 'em grow on the sticks." But Louie just gives him a sidelong glance.

"Okay," Benno says. "This here, he Alf. He gonna be here wit us. Paco, ya wanna show 'im aroun'?"

In a few hours Alf has become a citizen of The Space. He makes himself at home immediately and he is useful everywhere: helping Juan and Paco with the garden; helping to carry water; helping Louie with the barricade. He is also the communications system of The Space. He carries messages from one working team to another: "Benno say we gonna stop an' eat now." "Louie say ev'ybody come help heem wif beeg piece he gotta move." He likes this. Everybody needs him.

But Benno is alternating from high to low, high to low. On the one hand, seeing this busy community that owes its life, in part at least, to him, is wonderful and astounding. Look what we're doin'! All alone by ourself! he thinks. And there is this strange light and good feeling that continues to possess him when he is in The Space. But beneath that is still the feeling that continues to nag him: We gotta get those other people here. And a vision starts to form in his mind that is so real that he sometimes stops work and just grooves on it. In the vision, the streets all around have been cleared and the old wrecks of houses that stand have been cleaned and repaired. Scrubbed and polite people sit on their neat front stoops fanning themselves in the summer evening, and nicely dressed and scrubbed little children play ball against the steps. In everyone's hands is an orange . . . a big orange. Everyone is smiling. . . .

nine

A cat may stay in a dead City that humans leave and eat the mice that stay to eat the ancient crumbs. And there are enough crumbs in a dead City to feed an army of mice, and enough mice to feed an old homeless cat.

Standing on top of the barricade wall one morning surveying his domain—and that *is* the way he sees it—out of the corner of his eye, Benno catches a glimpse of the stooped figure, moving so fast that he is out of sight before Benno really sees him clearly. As before, he disappears suddenly. There is no way to pretend he isn't there. Benno has to accept the fact that they are not alone: There is someone who is here on a regular basis, just as they are. He climbs down.

"There that guy again, out in The Space," he says to Moon, as if he were saying "The world has come to an end."

"Yeah," Moon says. "We knowed he was here, din' we?"

"Yeah," Benno agrees. "I guess I jus' din' wanna think he was here so much."

"Where'd he go?" Louis asks.

"I din' see," Benno says. "One minute ya see 'im, nex' minute he gone."

"Ya think he saw ya?" Louie asks.

"I dunno," Benno says, "but I guess he gotta know we here. We ain't quiet. We ain't hidin'."

"I think I gonna go see," Louie says, and he starts for the barricade.

"Not alone," Benno says. He is the commander again. "I gonna go, too."

"You goin', I goin'," Moon says.

"Juan, Paco, Alf, Willie, y'all stay here," Benno says.

"Why I gotta stay?" Willie asks.

"Somebody gotta be in charge here," Benno says to him.

"Yeah? I in charge?"

"Fer now, y'are," Benno says.

Louie says, "We gotta go armed. Might be he dangerous."

"Come on, Louie," Moon says reasonably. "We got no arms."

"Yeah we got some," Louie says. "We got these sharp sticks I made. Now I know what they're fer."

"What we gonna do wit 'em sticks?" Benno asks. "We gonna stick 'em into some people?"

"Maybe we ain't, but we wan' 'em to think we gonna," Louie says, as if this were an everyday thing, and maybe it is.

Benno thinks this over and decides the sticks may give them courage. "An' don' forget them dogs is out there," Louie says. Benno is sold.

Carrying sticks and crouched like commandos, Benno, Moon, and Louie go out the back way into the alley and soon are seen by the keepers of the fort emerging into the street outside the barricade, moving quietly through the rubble, and then entering the street that is a continuation of their own. They explore the piles of debris, fearfully at first, but then gain courage as they go. The dogs, howling not too far off, add to the tension. And then Benno notices something: There are footprints in the dust, and an almost unnoticeable path, only slightly more cleared than the street. They follow it silently, nervously, trying to suppress fear and keep it invisible from one another; making themselves brave; forcing their feet to take them into a peril they do not know.

And then they are standing before a door. Well, call it a door: It is several boards, nailed together, leaning against an opening into what was once the cellar of a house. Now it is all there is of the house, all the floors above having been torn away, pulled down, burned out, trashed like so much of The Space.

"Now what?" whispers Louie. "We rush 'im wit our sticks?"

"No!" Benno says, a bit too loudly.

"Shhh!" Moon says. "He'll hear ya."

He hears them, all right. In an open space above the so-called door, there appears a face to frighten even wild dogs: long, wrinkled, weather-beaten, gnarled like a tree, rags for hair. The body that goes with it is unseen. Benno doesn't know whether to run for his life or try to stick it out as leader. He does not have to make a choice.

The few broken yellow teeth show as the man says, "Just what do you think you're doing?" The three, clutching their weapons, are surprised at the way the man talks—hoarsely, breathlessly, but his words sounding like those of a television announcer or somebody like that. "Are you going hunting?" he goes on. "If so, just what do you think you will catch? Rats?"

It's up to Benno. He knows that. "N-n-n-no," he says weakly. "We jus' come to see who livin' here."

"Ah, so now you've seen. What comes next?" The voice is now challenging, suspicious. "You're on private property, you know. This is my house . . . what's left of it. . . ." And now the man starts mumbling so that the boys can't hear him clearly: something like ". . . all my life . . . leave it now . . . pesky kids . . . trouble-makers."

"Whatda say?" Louie asks.

"What I say is certainly none of your business, is it? I have lived here most of my life. I have flummoxed the City. I have outfoxed police and social workers. And I'm not going to be put in jeopardy because of the intrusion of some hoodlums."

"Hey!" Louie exclaims. "This guy got 'lectric lights!"

The man is temporarily diverted. "Of course I have lights. Where do you come from? What do you think I am—a tramp? Any good house has electric lights these days."

"But all the 'lectric aroun' here turned off, ain't it?" Benno asks.

"Some is, some isn't. It's possible to obtain, but one needs the know-how."

"Well, we ain't got it," Benno says.

Now this changeable stranger becomes grandiose, boastful. "Well, you need skills. You need a touch." Now he pushes the door aside and reveals himself to be a very tall, thin man.

98

"Would ya show us how ya got it?" Benno asks.

"Why should I?"

Benno is stumped. He wants to say that, in pioneering, everybody shares, but he says, "I dunno. All we got's a flashlight and some candles. Tha's it."

"Ha!" the stranger says. "So you're just camping out over there, eh? Oh yes, I saw you come in. I've seen what you've done. There is nothing that goes on in this place that I don't know about." Now he clouds up again. "So exactly what did you say you were doing with those sticks?"

"We . . . we keep 'em fer . . ." Benno starts.

". . . the dogs," Louie says.

"Indeed?" the stranger says, not convinced. "I'll tell you something: Those dogs are part of my security system."

"Like how?" Moon asks.

"Two ways: Number one, hardly anyone will come into this area because they know those dogs are here. Number two, when anyone does come in, the dogs start barking and howling and so I am alerted and take care."

"Yeah, but they howl some even if nobody come into . . ." Benno starts to say "The Space" but stops himself . . . "into this place. They howl when they start fightin'."

"That's true, young man," the stranger says, "but it's a different sound. You get to understand the sounds. They have a language."

To Benno, this is life in the wilds. This is what pioneering is all about. This is man and beast, living side-by-side, sharing the earth. But he is shaken out of his meanderings by the stranger, who now has another mood change.

"Now, I'm going to lay down the law and you'd better listen," he growls in what seems a truly threatening manner. "I don't want anyone in these parts, at all, but the reality is that you are here now, and I'm not going to chase you out. Not now, anyhow."

That tees Louie off. He thrusts his face near the old man's. "Just how's an ole guy, like you is, gonna try an' chase us out?" he hoots.

Benno and Moon try to shut him up, but he's not budging. "We three could lay ya out flat," Louie boasts. Benno gives Louie a good kick.

"Maybe you could and maybe you couldn't," the man says.

"We don' wanna lay ya out," Benno rushes to say. "Louie, he talkin' offa the top of his dumb head."

"Well, that's good," the stranger says, "because after you lay me out, this friend of mine, name of Ironsides, is going to take over." And as he says "Ironsides" there appears at his side, as if by magic or a trick of light, a dog that looks for all the world like the wild dogs of The Space. The boys pull back in alarm. "Now, Iron came to live with me when he was just born. His mother left him one day and I took him in. He was a runt then, but you can see he isn't a runt anymore. One thing Iron doesn't like and that's if someone or something looks as if he or it is going to bother me. He doesn't even wait to find out what's the trouble: He just goes nearly crazy!" And the man shakes his head as if he can barely understand the behavior of this dog.

"That a wild dog?" Moon asks respectfully.

"Well, he *was* a wild dog, but I civilized him. That was when I believed in civilization. And most of the time he forgets he's a wild dog, but there are a few things that can make him remember, so I suggest you tread lightly when you come around. Do you understand?"

"Ya *bet*!" Moon says. "We unnerstan' real good."

"Wha's yer name?" Benno asks.

"Did I ask you your name?" the stranger asks.

"No, ya dint," Benno says.

"Well, my name is one of the only things I have left that's mine, and . . ." And now he's back to mumbling.

"But . . ." Benno starts, but the door shuts. Benno is thinking this part is not at all like the western movie he saw, or like his dream of neighborliness. "Inna movie," he says, "a guy say, like, 'Wha's yer name, stranger?'"

"Yeah," Moon says. "An' then maybe he say, 'Who want to know?' and then he pull a gun."

"Yeah, I guess maybe," Benno says, giving back some of his dream of pioneering. "Hey, we gotta git back. The kids be worryin' what happen to us."

"What did happen to us?" Moon asks.

"I dunno," Benno says, as they make their way through the obstacles of The Space. "I dunno."

ten

Fear hangs over the City like a low cloud that you can touch, but you try to stay beneath the cloud; you try to keep your distance. You try to get used to its being there above and around you, so that if it gets too close you can fight it off.

Waiting with Moon, Juan, and Paco, the next day, is a very short man whom Benno recognizes as Moon's uncle, Tio Chico. It is easy to see how he got his name: He is shorter than Moon, with a man-sized head and shoulders, long arms, but a short body and legs. Although he is small, his arms, in their short-sleeved shirt, look very muscular and strong. His face is twisted a little out of shape, but he has a pleasant, wide-eyed smile. He wastes no time.

"I got this feelin' you guys is up to somethin', so since I'm givin' ya the loan of some stuff, like a good flashlight, tools, and all, how about yez come clean wit me and tell me what's up?"

There goes the secret, Benno thinks, but he also

thinks this is a very appealing little man, standing there smiling but saying: It's time to tell me.

"I din' say nothin' 'bout it," Moon says, worried that it appears that he has ratted on his friends.

"He din' hafta say nothin'," Tio Chico says. "All the time I see three kids gettin' up early, stuffin' their pockets wit anythin' that ain't tied down, cuttin' out an' not gettin' back till late. So I asks myself, 'What kin they be doin' all day, ev'y day?' Also, I says to myself, 'Maybe they're like it better if I don' ask.' But myself says, 'Yeah, but maybe they're in some kinda trouble.'"

"We ain't in no trouble, Tio Chico," Moon says.

"No trouble," Juan says.

"What I gonna do wit 'im?" Moon asks Benno quietly.

"Can we trus' 'im?" Benno asks.

"I trus' 'im," Moon says. "He's a real okay person."

"I ain't got no kids of my own," Tio Chico says. "But I know how ya feel. I remember how it feels to have the old folks gettin' in the way. All the same, I wanna know what yer doin'. If it's okay, I don't say nothin' more, not nothin' to nobody, if ya don' want me to. If it ain't okay, I'm gonna give ya a hard time."

"Okay," Benno begins, "we . . . we discover a . . . a secret place, and we's like . . . settlin' it."

"Settlin'?" Tio Chico says. This is not what he expected. "Ya what? What'd he say?" He turns to Moon.

Moon takes over. "We, a bunch of us, we fixin' up a house . . . a real terrific house, Tio Chico, in a place we call The Space, but the real name is"—he lowers his voice—". . . Secret City."

"A house!" Tio Chico exclaims. "Ya kids took over a house! Ya kids squattin' somewheres?"

"Right!" Juan says brightly. "Ya got it, Tio," and he does a little shuffle, humming to himself and drumming on a tin can he is bringing along.

"Lemme think 'bout that," Tio Chico says, and he does for a minute or two. Then Moon interrupts his thought.

"Tio Chico," he says, "we ain't doin' nothin' bad."

"No way," Benno says. "We doin' real good stuff. We cleanin' up a place what was no use to nobody, and we givin' a coupla kids a place . . . a place to stay."

Tio Chico looks up at that. "Like how?" he asks. "What kids?"

"Well," Benno says. "A coupla kids we see stayin' inna alley, real steady, we give 'em a big place to live in, where they ain't sleepin' inna street or a ole dirty place where they gonna git ripped off an' all."

"Well, I dunno . . ." Tio Chico starts, drawing the words out in a way that makes Benno nervous. "I jus' don' know. I think I gotta see this place."

Benno is sore. What business is it of Tio Chico's if they have The Space or not? Since when is he boss?

"Maybe ya wanna know how come this is my business, huh?" he asks then, making Benno jump. What is it with this family? They all seem to read minds. Tio Chico goes on. "Numero uno, because these kids is my business, and numero dos, I jus' figure *everythin'* my business. So I gonna hafta see it. I gotta see it, but not now," he says, "'cause I gotta pick up a customer in my cab. But soon, okay?"

"Okay," Moon says, looking at his feet.

Juan says, "Ya gonna see the garden me an' Paco make wit another kid name of Ozzie."

"A garden, huh?" Tio Chico says.

"Yeah," Paco says. "We plant squash, we plant li'l sprouts, we plant potatoes, an' onions."

"An' there already a apple tree there—pretty old, and wormy, but there some ya kin eat." Juan is trying hard to impress his uncle with the splendor of this project.

"Yer not kiddin' me?" Tio Chico says. Benno sees this is the way to go.

"He's not kiddin'," Benno says in a rush. "They made a real good garden."

Tio Chico nods his head, thoughtfully. "So, okay, we gonna see," he says.

When they are on their way again, Moon says, "I'm real sorry. I din' think he gonna be like that. He never ask nothin' when he give us the loan of the flashlight an' the tools. I guess, like he say, he notice us a lot always goin' somewheres."

"Yeah," Benno grumps. This is his first private enterprise in the wide world and he doesn't want someone's half-pint uncle screwing it up.

They are well into the trip to The Space, not noticing too much where they are. Benno thinks he sees the little man in the beret in the next block. He has ceased trying to keep up with him—he's too fast—and has stopped mentioning him to Moon. Usually, though, he can keep him in view, and he imagines him saying "This way, this way," as if, by following him, they may avoid the Poison trap. Anyhow that's how Benno imagines it. So, now, he tries to steer his group over to the next block where he saw the little man—maybe it's just a superstition, but . . . This time it's too late! The Poisons have seen them and, having nothing more important to do, decide to push them around. They're big. It's not a fair match.

105

Moon and Benno yell "Run!" to the little kids, and then they start to tangle with a couple of the Poisons. We're going to be dead meat, Benno thinks, in the second he has to think.

And suddenly there's a screeching of brakes, a blaring of a horn, and a little man, brandishing a tire iron, flies through the air with a gymnast's leap and is on the back of one of the Poisons like a monkey and beating about the shoulders of another. "Get offa them kids, ya lugs ya," he yells, "or this one's head's gonna change shape. *Uno, dos* . . .!" The Poisons are off, astounded at this flying dwarf, and Benno, Moon, Juan, and Paco are all crammed into the cab with the passenger.

All Tio Chico says is, "Where to?"

After Tio Chico drops them a few blocks south of The Space, they make the rest of the trip in total silence, each with a headful of thoughts to be sorted out. But all is forgotten when they arrive at the house.

"Ho!" Alf calls, in his cheerful voice, as they enter the backyard. "I got a s'prise fer ya," and in his island sound, the last word comes as a sort of question.

"What s'prise?" Juan asks.

"I tell ya now, den where ees s'prise later?"

The four go in, but Paco peers from the window and sees what Alf is up to. He is walking around the edges of the backyard, picking out rocks. He takes a long time selecting them, picking up one, putting it down. Now he collects smaller stones and makes a ring on the bare earth. Then he starts breaking up dry twigs and dropping them into the ring of stones and lights them with a match. He reaches into his pocket and brings out a few handfuls of something that Paco cannot see.

"I don' know what he doin'," Paco says, disgusted.

Benno meanwhile replaces all of his other worries with a worry about Louie. Through with sharpening sticks, Louie is now making slingshots out of Y-shaped sticks and elastic that looks as if it came from somebody's clothing.

"Watcha doin' *now,* Louie?" Benno asks. "We gonna hunt wild dogs wit them, too? Or we gonna git the ol' man?" He doesn't mean to sound sarcastic, but he does because he's nervous. What does he know about Louie, anyway, he thinks.

"Augh!" Louie says. "Don' worry. I ain't gonna hurt nobody." But Benno worries. The responsibility of this city he has created is beginning to weigh heavily on him. In a way, he thinks, they are here because of me, so I am responsible for all of them and what they do.

From the window, Paco yells, "Look what he doin'! He cookin' somethin'. Firs' he kinda grind stuff up, wit stones, an' now he cookin'." They all take a look out the window. Alf takes what has been cooking and puts it aside. He drips a bit of water from his fingers and it sizzles on the stones. Then he takes up something and puts it on the stone. Steam rises. There's something cooking all right. He goes through this procedure several times, then he turns and calls up to the house.

"Ya kids want some corn cakes fer yer lunch?" he asks.

Louie rolls his eyes and swallows. "Ya bet!" he calls, and is first down the stairs.

"Dey ain't so very good shape," Alf says. "But dey smell okay." On the hot stones, eight flat, brown cakes await them. They can't believe it.

"How'd ya do that?" Benno asks.

107

"Well, I get dees corn, an' I grind eet a leetle wif dees stones, den I put a leetle water an' make eet jus' right. Den I bake 'em on dees stones."

"He done that before in the alley," Willie says.

"They good!" Juan says. "They verra verra good."

Benno can't get over what this small boy has done. He decides not to ask where he got the corn. "Well, ya done real good, Alf," he says.

"I learn dees from my mama," Alf says.

"Where's yer ma, Alf?" Benno asks.

"She die, my mama," Alf says. "She die when I am leetle. Las' year."

"Ya got a papa?"

"Maybe I got a papa," Alf says. "I leeve wif my papa an' den he lose hees job. Den we got no money for rent, so we go on de welfare, an' we stay een welfare hotel. We stay up all nights keelin' roaches. When he go out to find work, he tell me stay in room 'cause hall ees full of not good peoples. I stay in room wif roaches. Den he git job and we git kick outta dees welfare hotel, an' I be verra verra happy to not leeve wit dees tousan roaches. But we ain't got 'nuf money t' pay fer room an' food, so we go back to de welfare.

"So next time my papa git job, he make money all right, but he go to jail. He gonna be dere long time. So welfare lady takeen me to office and I seet dere alla day. Nighttime come and dey takeen me to 'nother place fer sleepeen. Nex' day, dey takeen me back to welfare office an' I seet dere alla day agin, waiteen. Odder chil'ren like me, dey seet dere, too. Nighttime dey takeen me to diff'ren' place fer sleepeen. An' same thin' nex' day, nex' night. Soon I thinkeen: Hey, what I waiteen here

108

fer? I ask true bone and true bone tell me take off, so I takeen off."

"You been on the street inna winter?" Louie asks.

"No," Alf says. "But many peoples do dees, so Alf kin do eet, too."

"We got roaches here," Paco says.

"Yeah," Alf say, "but dey ain't like tousand een one room. An' here ya kin go outta dees room. Nobody een hall to hurt ya. Nobody got a knife an' say 'Ya do what I say.'"

"Onna street there's knives," Juan says.

"Yeah, but onna street we ees together, us all. Ees more safe."

"I got a knife," Louie says casually, but perhaps boastfully, and he pulls his pants leg up and shows the table knife strapped to his leg. "I sharpen that knife and I sharpen that knife on the sidewalk, and that knife sharp 'nuf to cut any of them big thugs onna corner."

"Y'ever done that?" Benno asks, nervous again.

"No I never, not yit," Louie says. And he gets up and goes outside.

Benno and Moon start signing to each other. "This guy may be trouble," Benno signs slowly.

Moon signs, "No, he's just scared like everybody."

Benno thinks this has been not such a good day. It started with Moon's Tio Chico giving them the third degree; then he got depressed by Alf's story because it reminded him of all the other people out there. Now he has Louie telling him he's got a knife and is ready to take on the corner goons. He thinks there was more, but he can't recall it right now. He paces around

109

pondering these negative things, when another thought worms its way in and over the bad thoughts. Corn cakes. Alf's corn cakes. Suddenly Benno puts the bad thoughts away and smiles. Those corn cakes were good, but more than that, Benno thinks, they mean something important.

eleven

*The dead City may seem empty, but is it?
The places to hide are many; the places to
be lost are many; the places to be found
are few.*

*B*enno starts the next morning hopefully: Tio Chico
is not waiting for him; Moon, Juan, and Paco are
ready and loaded, as always, with odds and ends of salvage, either useful or edible. The day is bright; they
make the trip fast; the dogs are not in sight; and nothing
more has been seen of the old man in the cellar. But
things start to go sour when they arrive at the house: It is
full of smoke, and soot floats in the air. The house is not
on fire, but a small wood fire burns away in the fireplace
and a delicious smell floats on the air with the soot.

"What d'ya think ya doin'?" Benno asks, all the good
feeling of the morning ripped away. "This house look
like it's been bombed."

"Nah," Willie says, stopping for a moment from eating something he is holding. "We jus' havin' some of
these pigeons what Louie shot." And then Benno sees

111

through the smoke that birds are skewered on the pointed sticks and Willie is turning one in the fireplace.

Ozzie, usually silent, says, "Louie got 'em wit his slingshot," proud of his big brother. Benno hits the ceiling.

"Who tol' ya ya could kill anythin' in The Space?" he demands. "Who tol' ya that? Go on, tell me!" He is challenging Louie, who is half again as tall as he is.

"Who I s'posed t' ask?" Louis asks.

"First off, ya oughta know it. Number two, if ya don' know somethin', ya ask *me,* tha's who."

"Yeah? Why's that?"

"I say so, tha's why."

While this conversation is going on, the rest are dining on the pigeons, sucking the tiny bones noisily.

"Ho! Gimme some o' that!" Louie says. "Don' ya fergit who got 'em fer ya." At which Willie says in a high falsetto, "Aw, Louie, we din' know ya din' have none. We et it all," and then he laughs and pulls the pigeon from behind his back. "Oh, here it be! We got some fer ya, too, Benno."

Benno stares at them. "No, not me," he says. What kind of friends are these? Here he has found this home for them, started the settlement of a vast Space, discovered a new American frontier; and now this late-comer has the nerve to say to him "Who I s'posed t' ask?"

"I'm callin' a meetin'," he says now, still angry.

"Okay, call it," Louie says, shrugging.

"I called it," Benno replies. "This here now a meetin'."

"Here's what it's about," Benno says. "I wanna get ev'ythin' all straightened out. Now, this Space was dis-

112

covered by me." Moon clears his throat. "By me and Moon," Benno says. "Yeah, it was me and Moon who found this here house what you now sittin' in. Me and Moon got this place all clean up and fix up so we kin really live in it."

"Hang on," Moon says. "What 'bout Willie? He clean as much as you and me. What 'bout Paco? He make the garden. What 'bout the rest of 'em—makin' the wall, gettin' water, makin' things to eat. . . ." This is a lot for Moon to say.

"Yeah," Benno agrees reluctantly, "but they wouldn't be doin' that if we din' find the place first. We the beginners of it and we all say I am the president of it."

"*You* say you is president of it," Louie says, sucking a bone loudly. "Ooo, this is good. Sometimes I ketch pigeons inna alley. I cook 'em in a can. Benno, you boss me aroun', I gonna go back t' the alley. If I wanna be bossed aroun' I kin go to some ins'tution, like."

"Listen, Benno," Moon says, "s'pose we *eleck* ya the president, that don' mean ya kin decide what they all do."

"Tha's what a president s'pose t' do," Benno says, "decide stuff that is the best thing fer the people to do."

"No," Moon says, "tha's no president, tha's a . . . like a . . . a king an' like a dictator."

"So what we s'pose t' do?" Benno asks. He is deeply upset. Here he comes upon his . . . his people, eating pigeons about which he feels so protective. They are his pals on his lonesome rooftop. They understand about space: They fly free, coming and going from the teeming streets at will. Now, for some reason, the kids are trying to make him feel bad about . . . what?

113

"Well," Moon says, "if you a good president, tha's okay wit me."

"Me, I am a good president!" Benno says, mystified; how can they think otherwise! He has only the highest hopes for The Space. He has new ideas that would knock their socks off. Besides, he is the only one fit to be president, in his view. Moon, for instance, is good at ideas, but he doesn't have the . . . the . . . Benno cannot think of words to explain his enthusiasm, his ability to organize and, yes, lead.

Louie agrees with Moon. "Yeah," he says, "if you a good president, I don' mind, neither. But ya not 'llowed to say, 'Ho, ya guys, this here a law I jus' decided.'"

Benno thinks about this. There's something to what they are saying, he has to admit, but he is not yet satisfied. It is like he *asked* them into *his* house, and they ought to respect that.

"It ain't yer house, ya know," Moon says quietly, trying to explain, because he can see Benno is still worrying.

There he goes again! Benno thinks. Why is it that Moon seems to read his thoughts? Maybe because he learned to listen another way, with his eyes, and speak with his hands. Can he also see what is in someone's head?

"The house don' really b'long to none of us. We jus' squattin' here," Willie says.

Benno starts to protest. "Okay," Willie says. "Why else we sneakin' aroun'? You kids sneakin' in, sneakin' out? Why we blockin' off the street?"

"'Cause we wanna keep it a secret," Benno replies.

"Yeah," Louie says, "but tha's 'cause y'all know we git thrown out if anyone find us."

114

"That's the truth," Moon signs.

"Yeah," Benno says. "I guess you're right. But, Louie, I don' like ya killin' pigeons."

"I tell ya what," Louie says. "If I cook 'em, I gonna cook 'em at night an' ya ain't here. But we gotta eat, Benno. Us people gotta take care of us and the li'l kids."

Benno nods. Being the leader is not exactly as he thought it would or should be.

The days of summer pass into August without the citizens of Secret City noticing, so complete is their attention and absorption in the project. The city grows, not bigger, but more ordered, more like a home, a street, a neighborhood. Benno often thinks what a nice neighborhood it is: so much nicer than the real neighborhood they return to each evening, where the crowded streets now feel like a strange *world,* where the means of communication are totally different. There the people scream obscenities at each other; do rotten stuff; try to kill each other. And in the tenement, the sights and sounds are a torment to Benno though he has lived with them every day of his life . . . till now. The spell that he feels still settles on him as they enter The Space each day, and, though he doesn't ask, he thinks the others must feel something because they behave differently. Look how they keep working to improve The Space because . . . because they can see what is happening: Something good is happening. What is it? Benno thinks a lot about that and he thinks that maybe they all may feel this down inside of them where they don't actually think about it, but it makes them become different, even if they don't know it.

Nobody knows when they first become aware of the haunting howling. The wild dogs often set up a chorus of howls, but this is different—a long drawn-out wail of a single animal—and it seems that it will never stop; it echos in The Space.

"What d'ya think it is?" Benno asks Moon.

Moon shakes his head. "Sounds like a wolf, maybe like in trouble, by hisself. Ya hardly don' see a dog by hisself. They mostly in packs, even li'l packs."

"When ya ever hear a wolf?" Louie asks. "Nah. That guy in the basement, he got a use-to-be-wild dog. Maybe he be lock out."

"Yeah," Willie says. "Maybe the ol' man din' come back an' the dog ain't got nothin' t' eat."

"Yeah, well, you gonna be the one t' go find out an' give 'im somethin'?" Louie taunts. "Inna alley, ya keep outta other people's business. Maybe that go fer dogs, too." Having said that, Louie looks thoughtful for a few minutes, then picks up one of his sharpened sticks and says, "I think I gonna go see."

The others look at him and at each other. Then Benno, thinking of his role as leader, says, "I gonna go wit ya, but I think we gotta bring somethin' fer the dog t' eat, else he gonna eat us."

Paco looks stricken and says, "Don' ya go!"

"We be all right," Moon says, and he joins Louie and Benno. Willie is left in charge of the house and the barricades. He grows inches each time he is given this job.

The three take off. This time Louie is in the lead with his pointed stick, Benno and Moon content to let him head the expedition. In a few minutes they have crept up to the heavy leaning door of the old man's basement

116

home. To Benno, approaching it now for the second time, it appears more like a cave than a house, like a cave in the wilderness, and once again he feels the pioneering spirit come over him, bolstering his courage.

"I don' like this," Moon says. "I tell ya the truth. I'm scared. I think we shoulda took along Alf an' his true bone."

Louie says, "'Course ya scared. We all scared. Don' make no sense at all not t' be scared." Benno takes that thought in and feels stronger. Three scared boys are somehow stronger than one scared boy.

There is no question that the howling is coming from the basement, but how to go about opening the door with that vicious animal on the loose? Louie solves this by pulling the loose board door aside, just a few inches, and, at the same time, throwing in the hard crust of bread that had been dipped in potato water. After he does this, the howling ceases and is replaced by the sound of the dog tearing the crust with his sharp teeth. A bad smell comes from the basement and Louie puts his eye to the crack and looks into the electric-lit cavelike room.

"The ol' man's on the floor," he whispers. "He got one leg all twisted, like. That dog, he's right there beside 'im."

"He's dead?" Benno asks. "Kin ya see is he dead?"

"I'm not dead," comes a thin, weak voice. "Just nearly."

"What happen'?" Benno calls.

"Took a fall. Tripped over my own feet. Went crashing down. Something may be broken. Dog's been trying to break the door down, throwing himself on it, but he's all tired out now. He hasn't had anything to eat or drink for

117

three days." His voice fades as he talks. It is barely audible by the time he finishes. "You can come in," he whispers.

"Yeah?" Louie asks. "How 'bout the dog?"

"He's not going to bother you unless you try to hurt me." Again that warning tone in the man's voice.

"We ain't here to try an' hurt ya," Benno says. "We come to see why's the dog cuttin' up."

They have entered, and the dog does no more than whimper.

"It's not the first time he saved my life," the man says. "Give me a bit of water from the sink there." No "please," Benno thinks. There's a big old laundry sink made of zinc, such as are found in basements of old houses. Water flows freely from the tap.

"Looka that!" Louie says. "That sink big 'nuf t' take a bath in."

Holding the broken cup, Benno hesitantly approaches the old man while looking nervously at the dog. The dog rises and growls deep in his throat.

"Take it easy, Iron," the old man says, huskily, and the dog sits quietly again. "You fill his bowl with that water. He's dying of thirst, too." Benno does this and then goes to the sink to get another cup of water for the man. Moon holds the man's head and Benno puts the cup to his lips. Louie is pacing around the basement. It is rank with damp smells: dog smells, people smells, rotten food smells. It has a dirt floor, not a cement floor, as in the basement of the house the boys have possessed. This is, indeed, a hovel, hardly more than a cave, a ditch with a door.

"What d'ya think broke?" Moon asks the man.

"My leg," he replies, and his face is pale and full of

pain. Moon squats beside him and puts his hand on the filthy pants leg and touches the leg that is bent beneath him. The man gasps.

"Maybe ya need t' go t' the hospital," Moon says.

"I'm not going to any hospital," the man says. "I've been hurt before and I took care of myself. Ironsides helps take care." His voice fades again and he seems to drift off. "Here's what you can do," he says, rousing a little. "Get the door and use it as a stretcher. You can get me up onto the bed that way."

They do as they are told, Benno holding the leg steady as Moon and Louie lift the old man just an inch off the ground and move him onto the door. The dog is standing now and growling softly, making the boys jumpy.

"Stop, Iron!" the man commands, but weakly. "These boys are helping me. Sit!" And Ironsides sits.

"Now you can lift this to the bed and ease me off." It takes all the strength of the three of them to lift the heavy door with the fragile old man to the ragbag of a bed, then slide him over.

"Put the door back," the man commands.

"Okay, we gotcha there," Benno says, "but now how ya gonna manage?"

"You're going to set my leg," he answers. The boys exchange fearful glances. "First, go to the back of this room and find some wood . . . a flat piece about two feet long. Find two, if you can. There are rags back there. Tear them into strips."

"Why we doin' what this ol' guy tell us?" Louie whispers as they poke around in the back of this smelly cellar.

"Maybe 'cause he hol' the cards," Benno says. "We don' do what he say, he can sic the dog on us. We take

119

him to a hospital, he kin rat on us." But, he thinks, maybe because he is a neighbor in the wilderness, too.

"We kin knock him out without no trouble at all," Louie says. "He jus' a skinny ol' man wit a broke leg."

"Wit a big ol' dog which has got four good legs and lotsa good teeth," Moon says. They have found the wood and the rags.

"Now," the man says. "Over the sink is a bottle of stuff. You bring it to me."

On a shelf they find a pint bottle of what they all recognize to be whiskey, and they bring it to him. He takes it in gulp after gulp, and then almost smiles at them, relaxing, as it dulls his pain. After a minute, he says, "One of you stand at my head and hold my shoulders steady. You two others pull that leg as hard as you can. Don't stop if I yell. Just pull until it looks right." This is more than the boys thought they had undertaken.

"Yeah?" Louie says. "And what's ol' Ironsides, here, gonna do when he sees us stretchin' ya? He gonna jus' sit quiet?"

"Give him a dog bone from the box up there. He'll see you are friendly to him. Anyhow, he'll do as I tell him. Go on now before this stuff wears off. Hold me tight and pull like the devil." Benno doesn't know if he is more scared of performing this operation or of being attacked by Ironsides, who is still hungry after the little snack. "Come on!" the man commands.

And they do what he says. At his first cry, Ironsides stands up and growls. "Sit," the man cries, "sit, Iron!" and then he moans. And the dog sits as the boys pull until the twisted leg looks straight. Then, following the man's instructions, they splint it with the two pieces of wood and bind it with the torn rags. All four of them are soaked in sweat when it is finished. Moon takes a rag and goes to the sink and squeezes it out several times in cold water, then comes over and mops the old man's face. Benno gives him a few crackers from the cupboard, but he can't swallow them. They shake out some more dog food for Iron, who is whining sadly but not threatening. The man is drifting off into a sleep or stupor. Benno leans over him. "We gonna come back," he says. "I think ya oughta tell us yer name, now. My name's Benno. That's Moon and Louie. We yer neighbors. We should oughta know yer name."

"Name's Mc—" the man whispers, nearly asleep.

"Yeah, yeah, Mc what?" But the man is past hearing. They leave, putting the door in its former position.

"He say his name McWhat?" Moon asks.

Benno is too tired to explain. "Yeah," he says. "McWhat's his name."

"I dunno," Moon says, as they make their way across the sea of rubble. "S'pose that leg ain't set right. S'pose he needs some medicine. S'pose he get more sick an' we can't take care of 'im."

"Yeah," Benno says. "I been thinkin' like that, too. I guess then we have t' get 'im outta here an' call a ambulance."

"Yeah?" Louie says. "And then he gonna rat on us, ya kin bet."

"Well," Moon says as they arrive at their own basement entrance, "I guess we gotta see if he gonna be okay first."

They arrive to find the others worried about them.

"Ya gone so long!" Alf says, relieved to find his protectors returned whole.

121

"Yeah," Willie said. "When we dint hear the dog no more we figure he ate ya. Then what I gonna do wit these li'l kids?" He laughs. But when they all hear the tale of the old man's leg, they are clearly impressed with their expeditionary force.

"The guy's name McWhat," Louie says. "Inna end he tol' us his name." Benno figures it's not worth straightening him out.

"What we gotta do now," Benno says, "is git some food fer . . . fer McWhat an' his dog. I know we got all we kin do t' git 'nuff fer jus' us, but we gotta stretch it."

Alf goes out into the garden and gathers some green weeds that have been growing around the edge. Then he gets a bucket of water and pours some into a pot, which he starts to heat in the fireplace. It takes a long time to come to a boil over the little fire, but when it does, he throws the weeds in, along with a couple of potatoes and carrots and an onion. "Dees gonna stew a couple hours an' eet be a good onion an' potato soup," he says. "Dot onion grass, eet grow wild an' ees verra good." He juggles some green apples, a bit worm-eaten. "Dot dog, he hungry 'nuff, he gonna eat dem."

Willie says, "I gonna go back t' the alley today an' look at the dumpster an' some other places I know. Allus was plenty fer me, an' oughta be plenty fer the dog. Mos' dogs, they like pizza jus' fine. Even, sometime, there meat on 'em."

Now the attention of the residents of Secret City has moved from just the area of their house and grounds to the community surrounding, and in particular their time is devoted to food gathering and preparation. It becomes their primary occupation. Louie and Willie are old hands at scrounging and Alf had a good start at street living before he came to The Space. Alf, too, is a specialist in the preparation of concoctions of vegetables that Paco and Juan produce in the garden. As for the things that start turning up from their forages into the outside world of the barrio, Benno once again decides he'd better not ask where things come from. He uses several arguments with himself: People have to eat, don't they? How else are they going to stay alive? Is it okay to lift a few greens and things from the corner food stand if it's done to feed an old man and some kids without a home? It has to be. Even though he has spent his life in a neighborhood of elastic ethics, JoJo would always be the person to keep the kids reasonably honest in his family. Quiet, for the most part, he would boom like a storm if Benno's brother Jorge came home with something like a radio. "Where you get that?" JoJo used to ask, his voice strong, his eyes cold. And Jorge would know it was useless to say he bought it. Even if he had earned money, that money was needed for the family's food. "Nothin' in this house we do not work for. Nobody in my family steals. You understand that?"

Benno himself has not the nerve to steal. It is not only the fear of being caught or the guilt of doing wrong, it is JoJo who still stands by his shoulder that makes it impossible. And so while the others forage in the streets, he goes to a dingy market on the corner near his tenement and says, "Señor Lopez, I got a sick friend who got no money and he got a broken leg and he can't git no food. Ya got anythin' left over ya gonna throw out, anyway?"

At first Señor Lopez says, "If I give somethin' t' all the people that asks, I gonna be outa business. I gonna be outa business anyhow, if I have that much left over."

"But Señor Lopez, this ol' man he gonna die wit no food." He decides not to mention the dog.

"They all gonna die," Señor Lopez says. "Ya think ya the only one come in an' tell me that story?" Benno starts to leave, downcast. Can't Señor Lopez tell he's telling the truth? Look at this store! Cases of food everywhere: cans, fresh big red bananas, plantains, yams. His mouth is watering and his salivary glands ache. "Justa minute!" Senor Lopez says, as Benno starts for the door. "Here's a few things." And he puts into a bag some wilted greens, a couple of oranges, and some bananas that are going soft. He starts to offer the bag to a happy Benno when, seeing his face, Señor Lopez reaches up and puts in a bashed-in box of rice and a big scoop of dried beans. Benno gives him a surprised and grateful smile.

"Listen," Señor Lopez says, "ya think it's easy fer me t' always say no? People ask fer food, most times they need food . . . never mind why. Ya think I don' know that? Now git outta here."

Carrying his loot, Benno goes to pick up Moon and the cousins but finds that Moon has hitched a ride downtown with Tio Chico.

"He gonna do some acrobat stuff fer folks fore they go t' work," Juan says. "His ma she don' like fer him t' do it les' he hafta 'cause she feared he gonna git all broke up like Tio Chico. But Benno he says we need a li'l hard money to git ban'ages an' stuff fer the ol' man's leg."

That's Moon, Benno thinks, as he takes the kids in tow and starts for The Space. "He gonna be back up there soon," Paco says.

They run into Willie, who is emerging from his old

alley, loaded with banged-up, greasy pizza boxes full of who-knows-what.

"Ho!" Willie says. "Louie, he come las' night an' got some stuff fer the ol' man. He et a li'l, drunk a l'il. He not so hungry, but the ol' dog, he is."

Benno is jubilant to see that they really can dig up enough food if they have to. "I din' ask fer dog food," he says.

"There 'nuff pizza here fer the dog, too," Willie says. "Dogs like that, they gotta take what they kin git. Dogs like that, they can't be choosey."

Not only dogs, Benno thinks.

twelve

The City's sounds: metallic clanks of garbage cans being knocked over; sirens; chattering jackhammers; squealing of old brakes; rattling of battered cars; crying of cats; howling of dogs; running and leaking of flawed plumbing; moaning and keening of people and animals; and laughter—twenty different kinds of laughter—soft to loud, kind to cruel. City voices.

They have begun a new phase of their lives here. They all seem to sense it.

Nobody can really say what it is. There seem to be a great many routines and purposes that have brought a kind of order to the days. They go in teams to tend to McWhat, bringing him food twice a day; washing him as best they can and binding his leg in the fresh bandages Moon has bought; letting the dog out and feeding him; even tidying the filthy basement.

McWhat moves from sleeping to waking, sleeping to waking, many times during the day. He takes a bit of food when they offer it, but he hasn't much appetite. The dog Iron has become accustomed to them, and growls only when McWhat cries with pain as they tend him. Iron eats whatever is offered him, drinks the water put in his dish, but has little interest in anything but staying beside the old man.

Alf, young as he is, seems to know more about cooking than the rest of them, and brews soups from almost anything that is brought in: old dried ears of corn become corn soup; beans make a fine bean soup with onion grass, and with the rice from Señor Lopez's store it is a hearty dish. And it is Alf who feels McWhat's forehead and says, "Dees mon have bad fever. He verra seek."

They examine the set leg and find that it has developed a bad sore at about the place where the bone broke. Alf goes back to their garden to collect leaves for a poultice. "Dees verra good medicine," he says, "but maybe eet not so much good as dees mon need. Dees mon need some verra good magic, I tell ya. My granfather een island, he con walk on the back of dees man an' poison go out den. I don' theenk poison ees goin' out now. No."

McWhat begins to mumble. At first they think he is talking to himself, but it appears he is talking to them, at least part of the time.

"I was born here," he says. "This was a very nice neighborhood of hard-working . . .," and there is a long pause, while McWhat seems to go to sleep, but he hasn't. "Then it changed. Oh, it got so bad. Bad people, lazy landlords, but this is my house, my father's house. They can't make me move." Again he goes to sleep . . . or does he? "What they did." He suddenly starts again, quite loudly, and with agitation. "What they did, they

127

came with their big derricks and those big wrecking balls swinging, swinging, swinging . . ."

"There he go again," Moon says. "I think he sleepin' now." Not so.

"And they turn this street and all the other streets into an ash heap." He is muttering into his wooly beard. ". . . just garbage . . . out in the street." It seems entirely normal to these boys that this old man should talk to himself. A great many old and not-so-old people on the streets of the city appear to be talking to themselves a good deal of the time, sometimes quite loudly, and nobody seems to care. But why? Benno has often wondered. Because they have no one else to talk to? Then aren't they terribly lonely? Is it because they are half out of their minds from living in the streets? Are they poor out-of-their-mind people with noplace to go? Those questions are the things that upset Benno, not the fact that they talk to themselves. It gets him mad like the way he feels when he has to run to the roof of his tenement. These people on the street don't even have a squashed-up indoor place to live in, as he does.

McWhat is talking aloud again. "When they came," he says, "I went down into this basement." He is almost smiling, a cunning smile. "I barricaded myself with barrels and I stayed here while the whole upstairs came tumbling down."

"That musta been real dangerous," Moon says, awed.

"Dangerous!" the old man scoffs. "No more dangerous than living here was, before, with thugs, and muggers, peddlers of bad cess, and all that goes with it."

"He gettin' hotter," Alf says.

"Funny thing is," McWhat says, "when they pulled it all down, all the crooks left. This is the first time since I

128

was a kid that this neighborhood has been quiet and good again. I just live here, minding my own business. It's not a fine house—it's not even half a house—but it's my house and it's Iron's house. He and I like it here. Nobody is going to make us . . ." And now he really is dozing again.

"What we gonna do?" Moon asks Benno. "He prob'ly need a real doctor. The voodoo stuff ain't workin'."

"Eet not strong 'nuff ees all," Alf says. "Need stronger medicine. No leetle kid con make strong 'nuf medicine for dees man."

"How we gonna git a doctor? No doctor come in here even if we kin pay, an' we can't. No doctor gonna come nowheres 'cept to a hospital."

"We take 'im to a hospital, they gonna ask us a lotta questions," Louie says. "I know 'cause me and Ozzie go, sometime, to see our ma. They alla time wanna know where we livin'. We don' tell 'em, but sometimes we hafta cut outta there fas'. Anyhow, how ya gonna take that man to any ole hospital? He so long, and so broke up, like."

Benno ponders for a few minutes. The risk of being questioned scares him, too. But just suppose this guy were JoJo. Just suppose. He thinks another moment. "We *gotta* take him," he says.

They work for over an hour constructing a stretcher. The door, they decide, is too heavy to use, but Louie goes to get his longest sharpened sticks which they bind to-gether, and around this they lace McWhat's old and dirty blanket. McWhat has grown lighter in the days he has lain here, and they lift him without difficulty onto the new stretcher.

With Benno, Moon, Louie, and Willie each holding a corner of the stretcher, they start the long trek out of The Space. McWhat rouses enough to protest.

"I'm not going anywhere," he says, his voice rasping. "Not going anywhere, you hear."

But they ignore him and the procession continues, with Iron bringing up the rear. They expected, somehow, that he would stay at the basement, but he will not. He comes out into the sunshine, getting his bearings, blinking at the bright light of day. But he follows them at a distance and they think he will probably turn back before they reach the borders of The Space. Wild dogs bark in the distance.

Suddenly the distant howling and barking becomes louder and they knew that the wild dogs are coming closer. Even though they have become accustomed to the presence of the dogs, they are constantly aware and fearful of the danger. Benno tries not to show he's afraid. They all exchange sidewise glances to see if anyone else is scared. It doesn't appear so, so they keep going.

Now the sounds are very close and, without consulting one another, they hurry into a protected area behind a partial wall.

"I think it only one dog," Willie says. "I notice this sorta loner goin' aroun' sometime."

The lone dog is standing, now, in the middle of the street, poised on a mound of rubble, like a statue. And then the statue starts a series of low snarls, which grow louder and become punctuated with sharp and furious barking. The boys crane their necks to see the dog lower his head and draw back on his legs, vicious sounds pouring from his throat. And then they see Iron, who had fallen so far behind they thought he had returned to the basement. But he is suddenly there, opposite the loner, his patchwork body taut and ready to spring.

"We gotta get outta here," Benno says. "That dog gonna kill Iron and then he gonna come fer us."

They move as quickly as they can with the stretcher into the nearest side street, down some broken steps to the rubbled entrance of a cellar. They notice they have left a trail of blood that seems to have dripped from McWhat's leg.

"That gotta be why the dog follow us. Pretty soon maybe more of 'em come."

They cannot see, but it sounds as if the dogs are in combat; the shrieks are terrible. Louie creeps up the stairway and, lying flat, takes a look.

"I think one of 'em gonna be dead soon," he says.

The snarls, growls, and cries rise to a crescendo and then suddenly cease. Louie, still in his prone position, takes another look. "Only one dog there," he says. "Don' know which."

McWhat, who has not moved or spoken, suddenly emits a weak whistle, and in a moment Iron is standing above them. Here is a hero home from the war, bloodied, his torn coat torn even more. He is panting hard; a piece of an ear is gone; he limps, but he is alive.

"Good dog, Iron," Benno says, and rubs his poor head. The dog whimpers and puts his nose into McWhat's stretcher. McWhat lifts his shaking hand to pat him.

"We gotta go," Louie says, "if Willie an' me gonna get back tonight."

"Yeah," Moon says, "an' I gotta go back fer Juan an' Paco."

When they emerge from The Space, Benno experi-

131

ences, as always, the strange feeling of falling from some high place: from a roof, maybe. That's what coming out of The Space is like: falling into the world where other people live; back to the street full of peopled doorways, fly-covered trash, boom boxes carried on the shoulders of ragged toughs in multicolored layers of clothing; scribbled walls; in short, the ghetto, the barrio that is home.

Carrying an old man on a homemade stretcher through the streets might attract some attention in a small town or even in some other city, but not here, not in this city. They carry the shrunken old man like a load of wood, with nothing to slow them down, right up to the entrance of the emergency room of the hospital.

"What we s'pose' t' do now?" Willie asks, as he shifts the weight he is carrying. "We gonna jus' put 'im down an' let 'em find 'im?"

"No," Benno says. "We gotta see they don' throw 'im out. Maybe we gotta take 'im somewheres else. That happen once to JoJo. We hadda take 'im to three places."

"What happened then?" Louie asks.

"Then he die." For a minute Benno forgets what they are there for and stares into the distance, looking for a man in a beret: This is Poison turf.

"I don' like it, but let's go," Louie says, picking up his end of the stretcher as the others do the same. A social worker sees them and their burden and looks briefly at McWhat.

"Orderly," she calls to a white-clad figure, "please take this man to a cubicle and call the resident on duty."

"Cubicles all full up, miss," the orderly says.

"Find some place, do you hear!" There is exasperation in her voice. "And then come and tell me where you put him. Maybe you boys can give him a hand transferring him to the gurney."

Before McWhat is wheeled away, Benno touches his shoulder and says, "See ya." McWhat says nothing.

"You boys come with me," the social worker says, and she leads them to a little desk in a relatively quiet corner. "Okay," she says, taking out a form. "Whose relative is he?" Nobody answers. "Is he your father, uncle, grandfather?" She address them in Spanish. No answer. "Do you all understand English?" Nods. "All right, then, who is this man?"

"We call 'im McWhat," Benno says. "We dunno nothin' 'bout 'im."

"We jus' foun' 'im, like," Willie says.

"You *found* him?

"Yeah," Willie says. "Um, lyin' onna street."

"Lying on street on a *stretcher*?"

"Yeah," Willie says.

"No," Benno says at the same time.

"Why is it"—the social worker smiles—"that I seem to believe the boy who said no?"

She is pretty, Benno thinks. If she didn't have this label on her sweater that says MARIE LORRY, SOCIAL COUNSELOR she could be like a movie star. She is all neat and tidy and friendly and kind of calm. He thinks that sometime he would like to have someone like that for a girlfriend.

"Nah," he says. "We din' find 'im in no street. We find him in a empty buildin' like where he was kinda livin'."

"Kind of living!" She says it softly and nods her head and looks at Benno as if the words had touched something that hurt. "How long have you called him McWhat?" She asks them suddenly, surprising them. They hadn't thought of that question. Willie looks at Benno and Benno says, "Jus' this summer," at the exact moment that Willie says, "Jus' now when we foun' 'im." Benno looks disgusted.

"Why don't you two rehearse your act," she says a bit impatiently. "This isn't a game. This is a person we are talking about. I don't know what or whom you are trying to protect, but you are not telling me the truth. At least one of you certainly isn't. I don't think that's fair."

All around them, carts of people are being wheeled to and fro. There are moans, sounds of weeping, babies crying. Orderlies, doctors, nurses, all are rushing from place to place. It is like a busy street with a roof on it, Benno thinks.

"You don't seem like bad kids," Marie Lorry says. "My job is to help this man and help you, too. Do you want to help me do that?"

Benno speaks up. "Yeah, we wanna help the ol' man"—and we wanna help you, he thinks—"but we don' know much an' we kin tell ya some of it, is all, 'cause if we tell ya ev'ythin' we gonna . . . we gonna do some bad damage."

Marie Lorry looks solemn. "Okay," she says, "shoot with what you want to tell me."

"Okay, if ya don' bug us," Willie says quickly.

"No deals," Marie says. Benno thinks she's pretty tough for such a soft-looking person. "Let's begin with the address of the place you say he 'sort of lives.'"

"Can't do that," Benno mumbles. "Ain't got no address."

"That's nonsense," Marie says. "Every building in this city has a number and a street address." The boys are silent. Benno notices that Louie has disappeared without anyone noticing. Where can he have gone? Afraid of being asked too many questions, Benno thinks. Marie speaks again. "Is the building in this neighborhood?"

"No, it ain't in this neighborhood," Moon says hastily. If that isn't just like Moon, Benno thinks: always quiet with strangers, but ready to say something important that needs to be said, and listening, always listening.

"Then why did you bring him to a hospital out of his neighborhood?" Marie asks patiently.

"Ain't no hospital in that neighborhood," Willie says. "Ain't no firehouse neither. Ain't no po-lice neither. Ain't no—" Benno kicks him and he stops.

Louie is suddenly back. "It ain't a reg'la' neighborhood," he says, "an' that all we kin tell ya. C'mon, Willie, le's us git outta here. It jus' like allus . . . they ask you questions, questions, questions. But come time you ask them questions, they don' give ya no answers." He is challenging the social worker.

"C'mon, Louie," Moon says. "She ain't done nothin' t' ya." Louie turns his back.

"Don' mind 'im," Benno says to Marie. Benno doesn't want to answer the questions either, but he doesn't want to hurt her feelings. "Louie, he had a lot of trouble wit welfare people, but he don' mean jus' you, ya know."

"It's okay," Marie says. "I understand. People who are there to help you can make you mad because they don't seem to give you the help you want. But you have to understand, too, we don't . . . We are not always able to give you what you want . . . and need." She looks unhappy. "And *need*," she says again. "For some of us, it is very, very hard not to be able to. And if you have to disappoint people over and over again, sometimes you grow a kind of crust so as not to . . . not to get hurt. Do

135

you understand?" She touches Louie's arm, which he grabs away from her.

"No!" Louie is not going to let her get off easy with all that soft talking. "My mama she sick near t' die, jus' like that ol' man, 'cause she din' have no clean warm place t' be sick in. Weren't no place fer her inna whole worl'." He starts to stamp out of the room, but turns. "An' my baby sister, she somewheres else I don' know where 'cause they say me an' Ozzie too big t' go there, or somethin'. So don' ya ask me no questions. You gotta tell me answers, firs'."

"Has this boy got somewhere to stay?" Marie asks the others.

"Yeah, he has," Moon says. "He okay."

"You boys were good to bring the old man in," Marie says. "Not everybody would do that. In this city we are so used to walking by people without seeing them. You were good," she repeated, "and if you need something, look me up here. Okay? I'm here almost every day and some nights. I have to go now. I'll look in on Mr. McWhat. And, incidentally, if you find out anything more about him, relatives or anything, it would be a real help."

"Only relative he got is Iron," Willie says over his shoulder.

"Iron?" she calls. But they are gone.

"D'ya notice how she kinda looks right at ya when she talk, like . . . like what yer gonna say gonna be very important?" Benno asks Moon. "D'ya notice?"

"Yeah," Moon answers. "Yeah, I notice."

"An' she don' yell at ya much," Willie says. "She pretty okay." But Louie is still holding his distrust close.

136

She is just part of the whole system, and he has no reason to believe in it or any of its parts.

"I seen my mama," Louie says, after a minute. "She in that hospital. She a little better, now. Maybe she gonna be okay. She say if she git okay, we gonna git outta this city. We gonna go down south t' her mama an' live on a farm inna country. Tha's what we gonna do, if she get outta there. She say me an' Ozzie we gotta go right now, but I ain't gonna go leave her here."

They are talking so much that Benno fails to watch for the little man in the beret, and they are deep in Poison turf. Louie is hurrying even faster than they. Then, suddenly, there they are, the Poisons, lounging about the corner, doing their grungy business. And the closed circle of backs opens up, and the punk in the bright green hat with a feather steps out of the circle in his silver running shoes and calls, "Ho Louie, man! How ya been? Where ya goin'? Ya like fer to make a li'l money?"

"Nah, man," Louie calls over his shoulder.

"So where ya goin' then?" the voice persists. He has stepped out of the group and blocks their passage. "Well, lookee here! Ain't these the li'l nuttin's been spyin' on us fer the He-Devils? Why, yeah, I do b'lieve they is. Why ya goin' nowheres wit them li'l kids, eh, Louie?" His voice is tighter.

Louie is embarrassed and peels off from the group and steps aside to talk to Big George. Benno is nervous. Should they run for it? They wouldn't have a chance. He has to wait and see what's happening to Louie, anyhow. How can they avoid this gang when they keep switching corners?

When Louie rejoins the group, Benno says, "Hey,

Louie, them guys yer frien's? That tall guy, he Big George!"

"Nah," Louie answers, shrugging. "One time I knew a few. I ain't inta that stuff now."

"What kinda stuff, Louie?" Paco asks. As for Benno, he's afraid he knows.

"Ah, ya know. . . ," Louie says, ". . . runnin' errands fer 'em, helpin' do their junk. I already tol' ya."

Willie nods knowingly. The rest just stare at Louie. Benno is still nervous. He always has been a little uneasy about Louie, ever since the pointed sticks turned up, and the pigeons, and . . . He just hasn't been as manageable as the others. It is hard, too, to keep remembering he's just a kid, because he is so big.

"Hey, Louie, ya dint tell 'em nothin' 'bout where yer goin', right?" Benno asks.

"What kinda frien' ya think I am?" Louie is mad. "I ain't been workin' wit 'em fer a long time." He hesitates a minute, then says, "I seen what happen."

"What happen, Louie?" Paco asks, and Moon gives him a little shove that means don't ask so many questions.

"Ah," Louie says, "they all crackheads, druggies, mean. They get busted by the cops. They get all burn out. They get all no-good. I don' wanna get no-good, 'less I hafta. I wanna . . . I wanna . . ." His arms gesture wide and wildly. They all nod. They know. They all want to . . . want to . . .

They are halfway back to The Space to pick up the smaller kids when they become aware that they are being followed. They exchange looks, but do not break their stride. They know what to do: Never let on you know

138

you're being followed; just cross the street and stay out at the curb, away from the buildings; keep moving, but don't run because the other guy might be able to run faster; just keep your distance. Most of all, they know not to turn and catch anyone's eye: That is a challenge to fight.

They veer across the street and hug the curb, but they still sense the presence following them. Benno gets ahead of the others and then quickly turns and starts to walk backward as if he were talking to the others. Then he gives a hoot and laughs. "Look who followin' us!" he says. They all turn and, with a big whoop, they yell, "Iron!"

Iron, wild animal of The Space, never before in his life, perhaps, going beyond his rubble jungle, is quietly following them home. Home? Yes, Benno thinks, it *is* home for Iron, for Willie, Louie, Ozzie, Alf, and McWhat. And, in a way, it is his home, too.

"We got us a dog," Moon says. "I think we got us a dog."

Before he turns back again to resume his trek, Benno has a moment's worry. Is Iron the only one following them? He imagines he sees someone duck, about two blocks back.

When they arrive at the house, they find the little kids ranged outside looking for them.

"Wha' happen?" Paco yells. "How come you lef' us? We was worryin'."

"The dogs was howleen," Alf says. "True bone say something bad, man."

"We think maybe the po-lice, they pick ya up," Juan says, while Ozzie silently goes and hugs Louie's legs.

"Fer what?" Moon asks. "Why'd ya think someone pick us up?"

"No reason," Juan says, now trying to act as if he hadn't been worried at all; so that he would not seem like a little kid without the bravery to live in this city—this frightening city without green places and the blue sea of the islands, without air you can breathe and not get all choked up with something like smoke. Once Juan had asked his mother why they had come to this city. "Because we got no money to live in the island. We come here so we have food to eat, and a good place to live, and schools for you so you can learn. And then things will be better." "But we don' have no place to live," Juan had protested. "We livin' here wit Moon. We was livin' in rotten welfare hotels before." "Yes," his mother had said, "but it's goin' to be better." "How ya know that?" Paco had asked. Paco's mama had looked kind of angry, then. "Because I gotta know, that's how. Don't ask me any more." And Juan could see she was trying not to cry because her face looked just like his face felt when he was trying not to cry.

"Anyway, we back now," Moon says, "an' look who come wit us." And he points to the barricade where Iron now lies, scratching and licking himself.

"Den where Meester McWhat ees?" Alf asks. "Where de mon who have dees dog?"

"Well, he stayin' inna hospital," Benno says. "They gonna take care of his leg and give 'im food and stuff t' make 'im stronger. I guess ol' Iron, he unnerstan' that an' he gonna stay wit us in our house. Maybe he be a watch dog fer us now." Benno is feeling tired but mellow. It's been a long day and they carried that stretcher a long way. But he looks around the cleared area of their barricaded swept street and then out over

140

the rubble-clogged streets of the outer Space. And even with all its debris, it seems somehow cleaner than the world they have just been visiting, as if it has been purified by fire. It has come back from its long years of neglect and abuse, from being a slum to being a brand new world. It has died and been reborn.

thirteen

In the City
good and evil
walk very close
together.

*O*n the way to The Space the next morning, Benno, Moon, Juan, and Paco decide to stop at the hospital and see Marie Lorry and find out about McWhat. She seems genuinely glad to see them. It stuns Benno. Why should this nice and pretty lady be so glad to see them? He has not quite gotten over her compliment of yesterday—"You were good," she had said. Nobody has been complimenting him since JoJo died. JoJo was the one who used to tell him he was a good person, that he was going to amount to something. He hasn't been too sure of that since JoJo died.

"I'm so glad you came. I was afraid you might not," Marie says.

Benno looks at his sneakers and mumbles. "Yeah, we come." He wonders if he should say thank you. What do you say when someone is so glad to see you?

With JoJo, you didn't need to say anything, but with a stranger . . . "We glad you here, too," he says. She smiles.

"I know you want to know about Mr. McWhat. His leg is infected, and he is weak from probably years of a poor diet, so the infection is worse than it might have been. But he is being well cared for and we have every reason to think he will be okay. You can be very proud of yourselves that you helped to save this old man's life."

Benno feels a glow and a rush of blood to his face. She looks them over. "Have you boys had breakfast?" They say nothing. "Well, I tell you what: I'm just going down to the cafeteria. You come along and we'll have a little milk and fruit and muffins together."

They exchange glances. "We can't stay long," Benno says. "We gotta get back t' . . . but . . ."

In a few minutes they are all sitting around a table in a bright cafeteria. Nurses and doctors in white or green uniforms, some with matching caps on their heads, are at other tables. A loudspeaker calls names intermittently. "Doctor Shield, Dr. Shield, report to . . ." and a doctor jumps up, takes a last sip of his coffee, and leaves his half-eaten plate of eggs and bacon. Benno has all he can do to keep Juan from swooping down on it. Instead he just keeps an eagle eye on it.

"Now, who have you got here?" Marie asks, indicating Juan and Paco. "And where are the other two boys?"

"This here my cousin Juan, and this here my cousin Paco." Marie reaches out and shakes their hands, sticky as they are with muffin and jam.

"Willie and Louie, they had to . . . they couldn't . . . they somewheres else." Benno answers the second part

143

of the question. He stumbles around the answer, trying not to lie to this lady and trying not to tell too much of the truth.

"Somewhere else," Marie says. "Perhaps in that strange part of town where there are no hospitals, police, fire departments, and so forth?" She is smiling and she says this as if she is making a little joke, but it embarrasses Benno. She's smart, he thinks. He wishes he could tell her the truth. He feels he could trust her. Like Tio Chico. Hey! he thinks, he has to ask Moon about Tio Chico. What happened about him wanting to come up to The Space?

They are greedily sucking milk through straws, and Paco is stuffing himself with muffins so fast that Benno wonders how he can swallow it all. The answer is, he doesn't. He cannot even speak. Benno is wondering if it would be possible to get some of this stuff out of here to take to the kids in The Space.

Suddenly Marie's name is called over the loudspeaker: "Marie Lorry report to emergency." "That's for me," she says, taking a last sip of her coffee. "You boys take as long as you like. And stop in anytime. I'll have news of Mr. McWhat for you."

They are alone at the table now and they're all glancing at Marie's plate with its untouched piece of toasted raisin bread and an orange. Benno looks at Moon questioningly. Moon nods, and Benno takes the piece of toast and wraps it in his paper napkin and pops the orange into his pocket. When they have finished, Benno collects their leftover milk into one carton. It's not much, but it's something. They get up to leave, but a magnetic force causes their eyes to fall on all the food abandoned by the doctors or pushed aside by fussy eat-

144

ers. They are embarrassed, here, to be seen doing what they wish to do and would do without thought at home or in the uncritical alley. They are about to leave the cafeteria when Benno turns on his heel and heads back. Quickly he pours milk from other containers into the one he carries, scrapes good leftovers onto two paper plates and, looking the people at neighboring tables straight in the eye, he marches out, grabbing a napkin to cover it all, his face red but triumphant.

"They was gonna throw this stuff out, right? Since when ain't it okay not to throw stuff out?" And they exit to the noisy air of the city street.

At the corner, the same boys who spoke to Louie yesterday lounge, smoke, and horse around. They appear to ignore the boys this time, after a quick glance at them. Louie is not with them. They get all the way back to The Space and have dodged around the barricade before Benno becomes aware of a presence behind them. Benno signs to Moon, "Somebody been following us."

"Maybe just a dog," Moon's hands reply.

Benno turns suddenly. Street rules don't apply here in this, their own stamping ground.

"Whatcha doin', Benno?" Juan calls.

Moon takes his shoulder firmly and shuts him up. "He jus' drop somethin'," he says.

Benno peers slowly around the barricade. He sees nothing, and returns to the group.

"Ya find it?" Juan asks.

"No," Benno replies. "I din' see nothin'."

"Maybe it jus' one of them feelin's, ya know," Moon says. Benno doesn't answer, but he is thinking that he never had a feeling that wore a green hat. Maybe it's a mistake.

145

*　　*　　*

The feast from the cafeteria is laid out before Willie, Louie, Alf, and Ozzie.

"Ya know what," Benno says. "We don' have t' have breakfas' there to clean up the tables. Prob'ly they like it very much that we clean up the tables. We gonna stop there and do that ev'y mornin' now."

"Keep lookin' fer somebody what don' have time t' eat ham 'n' eggs, too," Willie says. "Dogs like meat."

Nothing is wasted. When the boys are through, Iron licks both paper plates clean and then lies down and puts his nose between his paws and closes his eyes. For a time, eight boys and a dog sit around a fireless fireplace, dreaming.

Or, perhaps, seven boys are dreaming: Benno is having a nightmare. He signs to Moon, "I want to talk to you," and in a minute they both get up and go out to the yard. "I'm sure I saw someone," Benno says.

"Yeah, but ya looked an' ya didn' see 'im," Moon says.

"If he kin follow us alla way here an' us not know it, prob'ly he kin hide, too," Benno says. He is deeply worried. He recognized the green hat. He's sure of it. "I think it's maybe the guy Louie was talkin' to yestad'y," he says.

"Ya don' think Louie tol' 'im nothin'!" Moon says.

Benno hesitates only a second. "Nah," he says. "I don' know why I don', but I don'. Maybe the guy jus' nosy. You and me, we gotta keep our eyes open." He is still upset, but he feels better after talking to Moon.

Benno now takes to ducking into the hospital every morning. Sometimes he only catches a glimpse of Marie because she is busy with patients or relatives of patients, but she has told him where McWhat is and he makes a trip to the ward to see how he's doing.

"Ho, what d'ya say?" Benno greets the old man. For his part, McWhat merely grunts. Benno's pretty sure McWhat bears him a grudge for bringing him here. But look at him! He's in a clean bed with sheets, a glass of juice is beside him, his matted beard has been clipped and combed. He looks like a gentleman taking his ease. Finally, today he says, "Where's Iron?"

Benno is delighted. At last he's said something. "Don' ya worry 'bout Iron," Benno says. "We takin' good care of 'im. We gittin' 'im good food, an' he sleepin' inna house wit Louie an' alla kids. We even give 'im a bath." He laughs. That had been a struggle and a laugh: Iron restrained in the big bathtub by three kids, the rest soaping him up and rinsing him with buckets. All of them were drenched, but Iron looked like a real dog, and his torn coat smoothed out really well. "He look real good," Benno says. "But he miss ya. He sometime go an' whine at yer basement door. So ya git better an' come on home."

McWhat just closes his eyes.

"We're worried about his spirit," Marie says. "He doesn't seem to care about anything." But Benno tells her about his conversation with McWhat today. "He care 'bout his dog," Benno says. "An' pretty sure he care 'bout his house where he live. Maybe he jus' scared ya ain't gonna let 'im go back."

"That's very good thinking, Benno," Marie says. She is silent for a moment, then she says casually, "Benno, you never told me where you live."

"Who, me?" She nods. "Well I live real close aroun'

147

here wit my ma and pa an' the kids, and uset'a be my granfather, but he die."

"I'm sorry," Marie says. "You cared a lot about him."

"Yeah . . . yeah, I care 'bout 'im . . . now."

"So, how did you happen to come upon Mr. McWhat, who I am pretty sure was poaching in some abandoned building?"

"Oh no!" Benno says. "That buildin' ain't abandon an' he ain't poachin'. He own that buildin'."

"Owns it?"

"He live there all his life wit his family. Then they pull it down aroun' 'im."

"And he still lives in it?"

"Jus' inna basement."

"All alone?" Marie asks.

"No, he got Iron."

"Who's Iron?"

"Iron, his dog." Benno doesn't know how it is that this lady has been able to get him to tell things he doesn't wish to tell.

"So he does not live near the house you live in with your family, but you do know where his house is?"

"Yeah, I do." He feels he has fallen into a trap and he would like to back out, but he can't.

"Listen, Benno, Mr. McWhat can't go back to a half-destroyed house where he lives in the basement. Not in his condition. He can't take care of himself now."

"Yeah!" Benno says, so mad at himself for betraying McWhat's house. "Well how come all aroun' the street is people who can't take care of themself? How come ya not so pertickler 'bout that?"

"Oh, Benno, I try to do what I can." She looks so terribly distressed. Now he could kick himself for saying

148

that, as if it were her fault. "See, we've got McWhat in the system, now, and I know I can get him some care." She sighs. "I can take care of one McWhat, ten McWhats, but I can't take care of thousands of McWhats. I cry about that."

She, too! Benno thinks. Not just me because I am a kid and can do hardly anything. And the feeling of guilt about spoiling McWhat's chances of returning to his basement bothers him deeply. "Hey!" he says, as the idea hits him. "What 'bout if I tol' ya I know a kinda family which gonna take care of 'im in a differnt house? What 'bout that?"

Marie is puzzled. "In your home?"

"Well, not in the house where my family is, but a differnt house where I got a . . . a big family, like." Now he rushes on because she is looking interested. "Plentya rooms in that house. Room for McWhat, room for Iron. Plentya food." He is not even wondering what the kids will say when he tells them he is pledging to take McWhat into their fold. He just knows they'll agree.

Marie looks surprised, confused, but pleased. "Well, that sounds just wonderful, Benno. I'll come out and look at it."

"Well, there jus' this thing I gotta tell ya," Benno says. "If I show it t' ya, ya gotta keep it a secret."

"How can I do that? I'll be making a report on the housing McWhat is offered."

"Well, it ain't that I don' wanna show ya," Benno says. "But it ain't jus' my secret. This secret belong to Moon and alla other kids, too, and it belong to Mr. McWhat. If I show ya, ya jus' gotta keep a secret, else I can't do it." His heart is racing.

"Wow!" Marie says. "That puts me in a real spot. I'm

not sure I should even hear this, now, because if I know something about you that I hear in my role as a professional, I have to act professionally, don't I?" Benno doesn't have the least idea. Besides, he realizes she is just reasoning with herself. "Listen," she goes on. "I'm working only a half day on Friday. Why don't we meet somewhere and I'll see if I can work out a way to hear your secret and not obligate myself as a social worker. Do you understand what I'm saying?"

"Maybe," Benno says. "Like ya got a diff'rent part of yer head t' listen wit when ya ain't in the hospital?"

"Something like that." Marie smiles. "Where shall I meet you? I'll come at about noon."

Benno says he'll meet her at a corner that is several blocks south of where The Space begins. She writes it in her little notebook, pats him on the back, and watches him drift off in the direction of the cafeteria, from which she has noticed him carrying stacks of paper plates of leftovers. Where has he been taking them, she wonders. To his family? To another sick friend? *To this other family he has just been talking about? Is it part of the secret?*

The next morning he runs into Marie on the steps of the hospital. She's standing with a tall man who has one arm around her shoulder. Benno feels a pang.

"Hi, Benno!" she calls. "Come over and say hello to my friend Pete." Benno has no choice and he walks over slowly.

"This is Benno," Marie says. "Benno, I'd like you to meet Pete. He's a reporter for the *City News* and Channel 12 TV." Despite his wish not to know this man with whom Marie is so friendly, Benno is interested. He has never met anyone who works on a newspaper. He has found it interesting, of late, to realize how many different kinds of things people do for a living. So he says a quiet hi, with his eyes on those sneakers of his.

Marie says, "Bye now, Pete. See you later," and goes on into the hospital with Benno. "How about a glass of milk while I have some coffee?" she asks Benno.

How weirdly different from his real life this is, he thinks as he sits at the cafeteria table with Marie. And which *is* his real life, after all? At home in the trap of his tenement? Up in The Space where anything is possible? Or here, now, with all this interesting bustle going on around him, sipping milk with a person whose job it is to help people? Not only would he like to have a girlfriend like Marie, he thinks he might like to have a job like hers. Because, look, isn't that what he's trying to do, himself—and Moon, too—to help people?

Last night, on the walk home, he told Moon about the plan to meet Marie on Friday. "I kin still tell 'er no," Benno told Moon. "I wanna know what ya think. I was thinkin' it might be all right to tell 'er. An awful lotta people know now, anyhow. Like what 'bout yer Tio Chico?"

"He gonna come wit me pretty soon, he say. Jus' now, he so busy in the mornin' when we go up t' The Space."

"So what d'ya think? Tell her?"

"Well, ya gotta be pretty sure she gonna keep it a secret."

"I don' think she gonna let me tell 'er 'less she kin keep it a secret," Benno said. This seemed so amazingly fair to him. So simple and so fair. He liked it.

So now, here he is with this interested person, drinking milk, just like all the adults—nurses, doctors, orderlies—and nobody is staring at him and saying "Who is that raggedy kid with the holes in his sneakers? What's he doing here with all us big medics? Why is he sitting with that terrific Marie?" And wound up to this high, Benno launches into the test interview.

"Marie," he says—and he tries to act casual, as if this is just ordinary conversation—"if ya knew where there was a big place wit room fer lotsa people in it, and ya knew there was all these people without no place t' stay, what would ya do?"

Marie looks at him in a startled way, and then she says, "Well, that's an interesting idea. Let me see . . . if I knew . . . When you say a lot of space, what kind of space are we talking about? I mean is this open country, or is it a town, or a city with houses, or what?"

Benno considers this. "Well, it like the pioneers had, 'cept somebody lived there fore and lef' all the houses broke up and like that." Has he told her too much? Her face doesn't answer the question. "Maybe a city," he adds.

"Okay," she says. "It's a city, with sort of broken-down, run-down houses. What would I do? Well!" She takes a deep breath. "Well, I'd have to have lots of power. Oh boy, would I! And I don't, so I guess you're not asking me what I would do, but what I would do if I could." He nods, but she is carried away already into Benno's dream. He can see that.

"Well, I guess I'd have to establish a kind of triage, first." And when she sees Benno's puzzlement, she says, "That's a word used in emergencies of importance and it means we identify and separate the people who need different kinds of help. For example, if we were talking about, say, the people in a war, we'd take the people who needed medical help first, then maybe the hungry, and then those who needed shelter. But now we're talk-

152

ing about people who have no place to stay. So first we have to find out why they have no place to stay."

"Yeah, but Marie," Benno protests, thinking she is going to throw up some obstacles to his dream. "Ev'ybody need a place to live. Don't that seem like the most least thing a person kin need?"

Marie looks closely at him and she extends her hand, for only a second, to touch his shoulder. "Oh yes," she says, "the most . . . the very least."

"Well, then after the tree . . . tree . . ."

"Triage," she says. "Okay, after that we know what we've got: so many families, so many people alone, those who are physically ill, those who are mentally ill, those who need treatment for other things. All those ill people need special kinds of care in hospitals, and that would be the first thing we'd have to do, even if we had to convert some space from other purposes for their care."

Oh boy! Benno thinks. Marie would really know how to do it. His mind had not run so practically as this. It's because she's learned a lot for her job, he thinks. But it's more than that: He can tell by the way she is talking, so fervently.

"Okay," she says, as if she has just gotten that all taken care of. "Now, those people who are reasonably well we'd question for other things. What can they do? Are there any carpenters? Plumbers? Anyone who has worked on a building in any way. And most of all, those who are young and would like to learn. Yes, that's it. I think that's where I'm going to get my work force for this, from the very people who will benefit. The strength will be in themselves. It will have to be. But besides that, I'd be going out and getting volunteers . . ."

"Like me," Benno says, following this plan as if it were a story from a book.

"Just like you," Marie says. "And I'd go around raising money from the city, and from wealthy people and organizations. And I'd ask for contributions of lumber and pipes and all that you need to build things. And then I'd get all the condemned buildings the city owns and fix them and put families in them. And when I'd done that, I'd build new ones. And if that wasn't happening fast enough I'd get out the national guard and have them help. And what the devil are all those army engineers doing in peacetime when they don't have to throw up bridges over the rivers and all that?" A voice over the loudspeaker is calling her name. "I swear, I forgot where I was!" she says to Benno. "I've got to go. We'll talk tomorrow, right?"

"Right," Benno says. He is in the clouds. His imagination, no matter how vivid, has never built such a terrific dream because he had no idea what to work into the dream to make things happen—only what he could do himself, and he knew that wasn't nearly as much as he would wish.

"She's okay," he says to Moon later that day. "I don' think she gonna say nothin' t' nobody."

fourteen

The dead City
sleeps like a cat
with one eye open,
waiting,
waiting . . .

*F*riday morning Benno spends in The Space with the
kids, sprucing everything up. Willie takes Benno
aside and says he is pretty sure someone has been in the
boarded-up place across the street, the one with its backyard facing their barricaded street. He's been watching
and he is pretty sure he's seen someone moving around.
He's scared, but he hasn't told any of the little kids.
Benno claps him on the back.

"Yer prob'ly right, Willie. I kinda think somebody follow us here, one day. I even think I know who."

"Yeah, who?"

"Keep yer eyes open. Next time ya think ya see 'im,
git Louie."

Benno is nervous about Willie's report, but he is also
preoccupied with this meeting with Marie.

155

"Now, listen," he says, "maybe I bring a person here t' see this place. I wanna make 'er like it, see. I gotta count on ya." And he leaves.

Benno is early for the meeting and he gets to the appointed place in time to see Marie rounding the corner. She is not alone. The tall man named Pete is with her. Benno scowls. The meeting's off, he thinks. He's mad at Marie, too.

"Hi, Benno," she calls.

He gruffs out a hi.

"Benno, I know you're upset to see Pete here too, but when I realized where we were meeting, I was really afraid to come by myself. This is a very rough area. I don't like the idea of your being here, either."

"Me!" Benno snorts. "Ain't noplace I can't go."

Pete intercedes. "I wouldn't let her come alone," he said. "She thought you'd rather have me come with her than not have her come at all."

Benno thinks that over. It's true. He nods. "Ya din' need t' be scared. I'm here," he says.

Marie smiles. "So what do you say, Benno?" she asks. "Do you want to call it off or can you trust Pete, too? I do."

Benno is full of conflicting feelings: He wants Marie, but he doesn't want Pete. He doesn't want Pete in the picture at all. He wants Marie's complete attention. There never has been anyone since JoJo who made him feel like someone worthy of attention. Well, if he has to take Pete to get her, he guesses he'll do it.

"I gotta trus' ya," he says to Pete.

"I'll try to be worthy of that," Pete says, and extends his hand. Benno shakes it, but he still looks suspicious.

"Well, here's what I gotta tell ya," Benno says. "Right

near here is the beginnin' of a big place where hardly nobody live. It's all burn out an' broke down 'cept fer some ol' beat-up houses and parts of houses."

"You're talking about the North Sector, son."

I ain't his son, Benno thinks angrily. He gonna keep butting in? But he continues after a moment as if he hadn't heard Pete. "One day, las' spring, me and my frien' Moon, we foun' a real good house an' . . . an' we fix it up fer some kids who was jus' sleepin' onna street. If I show ya, ya gotta keep it secret. Okay?"

Marie and Pete looked stunned. This is not what they were expecting. Some kind of a pad, probably, but not a . . . an organized . . . what? Shelter?

Pete says, "Show us," and Marie whispers a weak okay. Benno leads them through the several blocks to the border of The Space. "This here is the frontier," he says. "From here on is what we name The Space. We got a other name fer it, too, but it's like a private name." And he says this a bit apologetically because he had planned to tell her all. But now he has this guy Pete to cope with. Pete is holding Marie's arm to aid her over the chunks of concrete and other rubble.

"It's okay, Pete," she says. "I can manage." But to Benno's disgust, Pete hangs on, keeping her from slipping into an enormous pothole that lies camouflaged under a heap of light debris.

Big hero! Benno is grumping to himself. Heap big hero!

In the distance, the chorus of dogs holds forth, as usual. Marie shudders and looks anxiously at Pete. "Yeah," Pete says, and he says it in a warning tone, "those are wild dogs. I know about this place. Nobody'll touch it."

"Why not?" Marie asks.

"Politics. The money they would need for this is being used for twenty other things: developing the riverfront, building a new bridge, new courthouse, new jail . . ."

"There you are!" Marie says. "They can build a new place to put the criminals, but not the families out on the street. Maybe they should just go commit a crime and get into the new jail!"

"Come on, Marie! This problem is bigger than the guys who run the city."

"Well, they let it get bigger by not doing enough soon enough."

Benno has cheered up. It sounds like an argument going on back there. Maybe they're not such good friends, after all. "Okay," he says, "now we jus' sneak in here, behin' this wall."

Marie is laughing. "Look at this, Pete!" She points to a roughly lettered sign that Louie put up: DANGER, KEEP OUT. "*Now* they tell us!" she says. "This whole place should have a sign on it."

Wait'll she sees the house, Benno tells himself. Maybe she won't like it outside, but wait'll she sees inside.

"I can't believe anyone really lives around here." Pete says, and he squeezes around the side of the barricade. And then he sees the swept street. "Holy moly!" he says. "What the. . . !"

"Look at this street!" Marie exclaims. "What happened here? Look at the walls at the ends of the street! It's like another world."

"It's another city," Benno says, excited by her reaction. "It's Secret City." He doesn't understand how come he blurted that out when he meant not to. Now he leads them to the backyard.

"Can you imagine a garden . . . in here!" Marie cries, still wide eyed. "Look at that: those are beans." And then she sees where Benno is leading them to enter the house, through the basement window. "You're kidding," she says, hesitating.

"No, this is the way in," Benno says. "Safer." He doesn't say safer than what. But Marie and Pete crawl in after them and Benno leads them, pointing the flashlight at the floor, to the steps. Then up the stairs they go, and the kids upstairs, hearing them, throw open the door to the kitchen. Marie gasps. Benno cannot interpret that gasp: Is it good or bad? The kids are framed in the doorway.

"This here's the kitchen," he says, not knowing exactly how to begin the tour or the introductions. "Marie, ya know mosta these guys, right? 'Cept this here's Alf. He from Haiti. An' this li'l one, he Ozzie. He Louie's brother."

"Hello, boys," Marie says.

"This here's Pete," Benno says, staring at Moon, who is signing madly, "Who's he?" "Marie's friend," he signs back. "He didn't want for her to come alone. We got to trust him."

"Okay, Pete, tha's Moon there, wavin' his fingers, and that big guy's Louie, and the other guy's Willie. Now ev'ybody know ev'ybody else." Benno feels exhausted. He's breathing hard, and sweating. He goes over to the sink to get a cup of water. He takes the tin can that is his and pours water from the bucket into it. Then he remembers Marie. "Ya want some water?" he asks.

Marie says, "No, thank you. Do you, Pete?" And Pete shakes his head. Benno gulps and puts the can back on the shelf.

"Okay, lemme show ya this place," he says. I got to do it, he is thinking to himself. I got to do it. What if they don't like it? He can't get himself to face that.

And so the tour begins, though it almost seems that Marie is more interested in the children than in the building. This worries Benno, too. But Pete is paying attention to the building. "It's astounding," he says. "This is a house that could be put in good enough shape fairly easily: new wiring, some plumbing, plaster. But look, these are good pipes." He points to a place where the plaster is torn away and the pipes exposed. What bothers Benno about his words is that he, Benno, believes this house has already been put in good enough shape. Pete should see the tenement he lives in!

"Look at that. The toilet flushes," Pete says.

"Yeah," Juan says, "but we gotta fill it wit water alla time, ya know."

"Just have to make the plumbing connections," Pete says. "Doesn't look impossible." Benno sees Marie give Pete a poke with her elbow. It must be as he feared. She doesn't like it.

"Where can we sit?" she asks.

"Mos'ly we sit downstairs aroun' the fireplace," Willie says. "Or we got the stairs."

"The fireplace sounds good," Marie says.

They are seated, staring at the empty fireplace, and Benno doesn't want to be the first one to speak, although he is dying to ask what she thinks. On the other hand, he is almost afraid to find out. Alf goes out and shortly returns with a can into which he has put some of his little corn cakes. He offers them to Marie and Pete. Benno watches as they nibble cautiously at the edges.

Then, "They're marvelous!" Marie says. "You *made* these?"

"Yes, lady," Alf says. "I de cookeen boy. Dees tree,"—he points to Ozzie, Juan, and Paco—"dey de garden boys. But Louie, he sometime also cookeen boy when he ketch peegeons." Alf kisses his fingers and flings them wide to show his appreciation of Louie's contribution to their menus.

"You all live here?" she asks Benno.

"Not all stayin' here," Benno says. He is thinking, though, The Space is my home too, but he knows this is not what Marie is asking. "Me, Moon, Juan, and Paco, we got a other place we live wit our fam'lies. The others, they live here now. This their house, too. They all help make it from a dump to a good clean house. They all sweep it, an' wash it, an' clean up the street, an' build the barricades, an' . . . an' *ev'ythin'*!" He sweeps his arms around to take in the whole wonder of their doing and, as he does it, it strikes him even more forcefully than ever, just how much they have done, what wonders they have wrought . . . by themselves!

Marie is silent for a long time. Pete wants to talk, but she stops him. "Pete, I *have* to tell these kids that what they are doing is wrong, no matter how terrific we think they are. I have to do that first." Her face is so troubled that Benno feels great sympathy for her. He wants to tell her not to feel so bad.

"I gave you a promise, Benno, and I'm going to keep it. Marie the social worker is not here today. Today only Marie the friend is here. Marie the friend says what you have done is miraculous. You have made a home for yourselves when nobody was doing it for you. Don't think I don't know that is wonderful. But in the ear of

161

Marie the friend is the voice of Marie the social worker. She says you are in constant danger. You don't know how unsafe this building is; I don't need to tell you that the area is dangerous—never mind the dogs, what about blocks of cement falling off standing buildings!"

"Marie," Benno says, "listen! In the street I live, hunks from the buildin's fall inta the street lotsa times. Nobody tell us, 'Hey, ya can't live here nomore.'" He almost laughs. "An' dogs! We got rats big as dogs in the houses on my street. An' they bite!"

Paco holds his foot in his arms and screws up his face. "Ai, do they bite!"

"I know," she says. "I know that. Pete, if these kids can do this much with nothing but their hands, can you *imagine* what could be done to this area with some tools, and a work force!"

"I sure do," Pete says. "All you have to do is get everybody's attention, fight city hall, raise millions of bucks, and . . . Wait a minute! *Wait a minute!* Now don't keep poking me, Marie! Let me talk. I could get a lot of attention focused on this, if you'd let me, and if the kids will release you from your pledge."

"What are you saying?" Marie asked. "You don't mean you want to spread this over the newspaper!"

"Well, not *spread* it, but how about an article that tells about kids who make a home for themselves when all the city can offer is infested and dangerous welfare hotels or impossibly crowded and equally dangerous shelters."

Benno is nearly out of his mind. "What? You gonna rat on us! I shouldna let ya come. I knew it."

"Listen," Pete says. "I'm not going to do anything you don't want me to."

"We don' wan' ya t'," Benno says forcefully.

"Won't anyone listen for a minute!" Pete says, annoyed. "Just hear me out. You want the same thing I want: to get a place for homeless people to stay. Right?"

Benno nods. "But—"

"Don't but me yet," Pete says. "Now, I wouldn't say where in the city this is. I'd just say what I told you. It wouldn't name you; it wouldn't name the area; but it could be very forceful in embarrassing the city into doing more. Most of what they are doing now is just providing temporary housing. We'll talk about permanent housing of a kind that could change people's lives."

"Already change my life," Alf says. "I leev een beeg houz. We gonna name dees street, den we gonna have a address, too. Gonna go t' school, soon as I con git some clothes, too, an' leetle extra money fer notebook, ya know."

Marie turns away. Her voice sounds like she has a cold when she says, "These can't be the only children capable of this. Benno, this is the place you meant when you asked me what I would do if I had a big space with room for lots of people, right? And my big plans with the national guard and the army engineers . . . you didn't tell me *you were doing it already.*"

Benno ducks his head. She is embarrassing him. The look in her eyes is so warm. There has never been another adult in his life with whom he has exchanged so much conversation, except JoJo. There has never been a person who has taken such close notice of what he has done, and done well. But now he does not like what she is saying.

"But, look, we came here to see where you propose to take Mr. McWhat. I don't know how to handle my problem with the two Maries—friend, social worker—but

163

neither of them could agree to this place. He is an old, sick man. He couldn't live here."

"He live here all his life," Benno says.

"In this house?" Marie gasps.

"No, somewheres else, not near as good."

"Not near," Willie says.

"Show us?"

Benno looks at Moon. Moon is signing "no way."

"Can't," Benno says. "We ain't gonna rat on McWhat. Ya don' wan' 'im to stay here, ya ain't gonna let 'im stay there neither. *'Specially* not there."

"You have to understand," Marie says, seeing Benno's downcast look. "This is not safe for you, and it is certainly not safe for him. Anyhow, how could you get him in—through that cellar window?"

"We could get 'im in. Don' worry," Louie says.

"Well, it doesn't matter. It wouldn't be permitted. I made you a promise, so I can't do anything about seeing this house, even though I know I should. But I have to say again that this is very dangerous: the dogs, the condition of the buildings, the area, the unsanitary conditions . . ."

Benno is confused. "But I thought ya liked it," he says. "I thought ya said we done good."

"You did. Oh yes, you *did*! You did something wonderful, but it still isn't safe, not the way it is. But what Pete is saying is that maybe this area could be *made* safe by doing what you did in a big way, with professionals doing it—the way we talked about when you asked me what I'd do. I'm going to start working on that idea immediately . . . just *start,* if it's all I ever do in my life."

She is looking into the faces of eight sullen or angry children. "Sorry I brung ya here," Benno says. He looks at Moon and signs, "Sorry." He says, "Sorry," to the

164

rest of the kids. He feels terrible, disappointed, and frantic. Is she going to spoil Secret City for them?

Marie sees what's happening. "Kids," she begs, "it's warm now. Do you know how cold it's going to be in the winter?"

"Listen," Louie says, "ya ever sleep onna street inna winter?" Marie shakes her head. "Lemme tell ya somethin', then. No matter how cold this house gonna git, ain't gonna git near as cold as the sidewalk in winter. That cold sidewalk, it eat right through all the newspapers and covers ya kin git. Ya kin near hear yer bones crack."

"See, kids," Pete says, "you think all you have to do is get water and heat in here, maybe some electricity. But there's more to it than that. A fire engine has to be able to get through these streets—"

"Can't do that 'less it kin fly," says Willie.

"—all kinds of emergency equipment. The houses that are standing need to be gutted and made stronger. New buildings need to be planned and built—a hospital, a school. This is a job for the city, not for a handful of boys, even with the best will in the world."

"Then the city oughta've did somethin'," Benno says. "They got alla people like me an' Moon squeezed together, where we live. Then they got all them folks ya kin see witout no place at all, jus' lyin' aroun' the street. An' kids like Louie an' Willie, din' have no place at all . . ."

"Hol' on," Willie says proudly. "I gotta place inna alley. Bes' place inna alley."

"But you're squatting here," Pete says. "You're squatting on city property. It's against the law."

"Ha!" Willie says. "Then we fixin' this house up fer the city. Look what we already done! We improvin' this prop'ty fer the city an' we ain't chargin' 'em fer it."

Marie and Pete laugh. Pete gives Willie a friendly pat on the shoulder, and Willie looks pleased. They all seem more relaxed. Except Louie.

"Listen," Louie says, back to himself for the moment. "Don' tell me 'bout the law an' all that. Ya think I don' know the law inna city? Inna city, if ya stay in a place, nobody better try an' take it 'less they bigger'n ya, an' kin beat ya up. Tha's the way it go inna alley, and the alley parta the city." He is so confident in this belief that they all just look at him, half-convinced. Willie and Alf are nodding their heads; they are young, but they are old enough to know this law of the city.

"I've got to think about what can be done," Marie says. "I can make a decision about Mr. McWhat: We can find someplace where he can be comfortable while he recuperates. But there's a lot to think about here. I'll come back, if you'll let me. Let's see. I'll try to make it a week from Wednesday, after work."

"Jus' ya remember, don' think 'bout nothin' tha's gonna be bad fer The Space," Benno says.

"Benno, kids, I promise not to do anything to hurt you," Marie says.

"I promise that, too," Pete says.

Benno isn't so sure. Lots of times adults do things they think are good for you, only you don't think they are. He looks at the other kids for their reaction. They all nod or shrug. Right now, taking a vote is a relief. Making decisions is getting very hard. Being a leader is a very big deal. But, on the other hand, leadership now lies more comfortably on his shoulders. It no longer feels like a weighty board. He notices, too, that he does not feel he must run for the roof.

fifteen

*The City has many voices and sometimes
they all speak at once. The City newspaper
is one of its voices. It can tell you what has
happened, and it can also help make things
happen when it speaks.*

The next week passes slowly for Benno. He tries to
pretend to himself that everything is as it has always
been, but deep inside he knows it isn't. There is an un-
comfortable, unsettled feeling, and by the end of the
week, he is so restless that he says to Moon, "I think we
oughta git started on a other house, even if . . ." and he
can't face the even if, so he just skips it. They have all
agreed before that the next one to tackle is the one on
the other side of the street; the one with its back toward
theirs. Even though the back is not as good as theirs, the
front is pretty good and they'd be able to extend the
barricade to it.

"Anyhow, Benno says, "we kin git a start on it, and
then we kin git s'more kids t' live in there and help do
the work."

167

"Tha's a good idea," Willie says. "Then there gonna be more of us inna neighborhood. Too many ain't so good. Not 'nuf, not so good neither."

Moon has wandered over to the window, and he gasps.

"Come look!" he signs to Benno.

Benno jumps up and joins Moon at the window, which, though still covered by the shutter, allows them to view the street through the cracks between the boards. What he sees startles him. Louie is in the street in front of the other house, and, behind a pile of rubble, a bright green hat can be seen. Louie seems to be talking to the hat. It seems to be just sitting there on top of the rubble. Now they see Louie make a violent move, reaching in behind the rubble and dragging out the head that goes with the hat. The hat falls off and Louie starts to pound on the head. Then suddenly Louie is tossed back, and a tall kid, whom Benno recognizes as Big George, jumps him and gives him a solid punch in the nose.

Benno's heart sinks. "Tha's the guy follow us here the other day. Ya 'member, I din' see him after we got here? Wha's Louie doin' wit 'im?"

Moon doesn't answer and Benno doesn't expect an answer. Now they see Louie rising to his feet, rubbing his nose with his arm, scowling, and shaking his fist at the guy in the green hat. And that kid is laughing! Then he ducks away. Louie sits down on a pile of rubble with his head in his hands.

Benno and Moon exchange looks and both make for the stairs. They are out of the house and around to the street in a few seconds, and they dash down the swept street to Louie, who is still sitting on the pile of debris. They slow down as they approach him.

"Whatcha doin', Louie?" Benno asks, trying to act casual. Louie looks awful when he raises his head. He looks like he might cry, and his nose is bleeding.

"Ah, nothin'," he says. "I jus', like, fell."

"Ya like fell!" Benno says roughly. He wants to flatten Louie but Louie is twice his size.

"Yeah," Louie says. "Tripped over this here junk." And he kicks the pile with his foot, nearly bare in its torn sneaker, and then grabs his toe.

"Yer lyin', Louie," Benno yells. "We seen ya talkin' to the goon in the green hat—that guy ya was talkin' to onna street the day we took McWhat to the hospital. So don' make up no story. Ya ratted. Go on, admit it, ya rat, ya ratted!" Benno is screaming at him. He sees The Space dissolving into nothing because this big kid, whom he took in and trusted, has betrayed him. And why? "Why ya gonna go an' do a thing like that?" he almost cries.

"Hones', Benno," Louie says, still holding his arm up to his bruised nose. "I dint rat on ya. I dint." And tears are, indeed, rolling out of the eyes of this over-grown child who is almost as big as a mid-sized man, but who is not one. "I dunno how he got here. Maybe he follow us that day. I know it my fault 'cause it me he after. It me he want. So prob'ly he follow to find out where I at."

Benno starts to scream at him again, but Moon holds his hand up and says, "Wait a minute. Why ya think he lookin' fer ya?" he asks Louie.

"I tol' ya, I use t' work fer 'im an' his rotten pals. Now he wan' me t' work some more."

"So ya tell 'im no, right?" Moon says.

"Yeah, but he say . . . he say . . ."

"Come on," Benno says, still worked up. "What he say?"

"He say I gotta do it else he gonna git Ozzie." Louie looks haunted.

"Ozzie! That li'l kid! What good he gonna be?"

"So I tell 'im I gonna kill 'im if he touch Ozzie an' . . ."

"Yeah, yeah," Benno urges.

"I don' really wanna tell ya this," Louie says.

"Tell it," Moon says quickly, before Benno can snarl something more at Louie.

"He say I don' work fer 'im, he gonna blow the whistle on all us kids here."

Benno nearly explodes. All this talking and he's right—The Space is at stake. This kid has betrayed them.

"It ain't yer fault," Moon is saying to Louie.

"Whatcha mean it ain't 'is fault!" Benno says. "Whose fault it?"

"Ain't nobody's fault," Moon says. "Louie can't help it if some goon see 'im onna street. He don' wanna work fer 'im. It ain't 'is fault."

Now Benno is mad at Moon, too. In a way, he is keeping Benno from giving Louie the punch he deserves. He has forgotten for just a second who could flatten whom.

"Yeah, it my fault," Louie keeps saying, and, while Benno can't understand just why, this is making him even madder. "If he don' see me onna street, he ain't gonna come foller me."

"Can't help that," Moon says. "Come on, we all goin' back t' the house. Maybe nothin' gonna happen."

Moon and Louie walk together and Benno scuffs along behind. He can't figure out just what's going on, but he

170

knows he doesn't like it. Moon is taking Louie's side against him. Isn't he? He stops for a minute. What *is* Moon doing? He stays there scuffing his sneakers around in the dust, going over and over what has happened and, while he can't exactly figure it out, his anger at Louie ebbs, and he returns to the house cooled off.

Louie now takes up a position at the front window, looking out through the cracks in the shutter. His nose is sore. It is not broken, but something else seems to be. He's very quiet. He looks scared. Finally, he says to Benno, "Ya wanna kick me outta here, ya kin. That Big George wit the green hat, he stashin' stuff someplace over there. I seen 'im. That what he wan' me fer—t' run that stuff aroun' fer 'im."

"We not kickin' ya out," Benno finally says. "What kinda stuff?"

"I 'spect it the usual kinda stuff," Louie says.

"Wha's usual?" Juan asks.

"Aah, c'mon! Ya know: radios, watches, and then bad stuff—smack, crack, sizzle an' pop. Cops know all their spots down there. Can't put nothin' inta storage inna neighborhood, Big George say. They don' wanna git caught holdin' it, so they gonna put it up here. They don' care we git caught holdin' it."

Louie has never seemed more dejected since they met him. Even straight from the alley, he was upbeat, but today, for all in Secret City, there is gloom.

A few days later, when Benno stops by the hospital, he sees Marie waving to him across the cafeteria. He is embarrassed to be seen salvaging food, but he goes over to her.

"Look what's in the paper," she says, with excitement in her voice. And there it is:

171

Benno feels weak and angry. "Pete!" he says. "He ratted on us."

"Oh no, Benno!" Marie rushes to explain. "Wait till you read it. He doesn't say who you are or where you are. It's the idea of what you're *doing*. He treats you with respect. Take the time to read it. Here, you may take this paper with you. Don't get mad until you know what you're getting mad about. This is a terrific thing and you're helping to start it. Just wait and see. I hope to see you Wednesday." Benno takes the paper and stomps away. You can't rely on anyone, he is thinking. Nobody. Not even someone like Marie. And this feels to him like a grief, like a loss, like a death. Just at this moment, it seems like everything's going bad. Try to do something and then somebody wants to stop you.

Back in The Space with the newspaper spread out, Benno reads aloud, slowly, to the kids, stumbling over some of the big words:

> Eight children, who somehow have fallen between the cracks of the welfare system, have established a home for themselves in one of the derelict sections of this city. Cleaning, scrubbing, building, planting—these kids have done it all, and by themselves, because others won't or can't, for some reason or other, do it for them.

And the article goes on to describe the house in detail and the things they have done to make it livable. "This is the first in a series," the article finishes up.

"Hey, that ain't so bad," Moon says, after a moment's

thought. "He din' say it was us. He din' say where The Space is." A murmur of agreement goes through the group and Benno reads it over to himself. Maybe it's okay. Anyhow, he feels better.

The next day Marie is waiting with the second article. This time Benno does not stamp away. Okay, he'll wait and see before he gets mad.

NOT A PALACE, BUT KIDS' HOME IS NOT A CITY SHELTER

Eight children have settled a barren quarter of this city, like the pioneers who settled this country.

"Ya hear that!" Benno exclaims. "Pioneers. That what I say we are! He say the same thing!"

Needing a home, these kids have set up a small, idealistic (though not ideal) community. In reporting this story, this reporter in no way suggests that this is a good way for children to live. On the contrary. What we hope to do in this series is call attention to the need for *immediate* action to establish *permanent housing* and professional care for the homeless people of all ages who populate the streets—men, women, and children, individuals and families. The question is asked, "Why are these people homeless?" And our answer is: "Many reasons, but none of them matter. *They are homeless!*" That is the immediate problem, and that is the problem that must be solved *now*. The whys can be addressed next. A private citizens' commission is being organized by outstanding, able, generous people, responding to yesterday's article.

"We famous!" Willie says. "We're in the paper jus' like other folks git their names in the paper. Benno, ya let me read that paper when ya finish?"

Benno hands the paper to Willie. In the evenings, when he leaves to go back to the old neighborhood with Moon and the cousins, Willie is usually poring over the newspapers that have collected with the rest of the salvage. "Our names ain't in the paper," he says.

"What all ya find t' read in the newspaper, Willie?" Moon asks.

"Ev'ythin'. I learnt t' read from the newspaper. See them great big letters. They make it easier. Now I read the little letters, too. It take time, but I gittin' better. Ya read it a lot, it gits like a story. One day it tell ya somethin'. Nex' day it tell ya more. Look here! Ya 'member 'bout that garbage boat? That boat still goin' aroun' the worl', aroun' the worl', an' nobody don' let 'em dump the garbage this whole summer since we bin here. Ev'y day they tell ya more 'bout it. How ya think that gonna end? They gotta find somewheres." Willie folds himself into a squat and dives into more stories about other people all around the earth. In the newspaper, Willie's world is very large.

sixteen

*There can be
no great City
where the citizens
do not aspire.*

In the days that follow, Louie can be seen standing at the window, scowling. His bad feelings from his encounter with Big George have left him despondent. He tells Benno, "My mama, she done drugs, then drugs done her. Why I work fer Big George, and his boss before him, was fer t' git my mama what she need. Then she near die inna street."

"She O.D.?" Willie asks.

"No, she ketch noomona sleepin' inna street. But she gittin' better. She say no more drugs, no more street. We all goin' back down south to 'er mama. It ain't a big farm or nothin': jus' like a li'l house wit a veg'able garden, a pig, chickins. We gonna like that."

"That soun' good," Willie says. "Louie, that soun' real real good." And for a while Louie will look better, but then he sinks again.

175

"Benno," he says, "I gotta go work fer Big George or he gonna do us bad. I gotta take the chance. If they catch me, I gotta ask ya a favor: take Ozzie to my ma inna hospital. Okay?"

"No okay!" Benno says. "Yer not gonna work fer that scum bum. Ya quit. Now ya gotta stay quit." He doesn't know where these words come from because, deep down inside, he is still very upset about Louie being the one who led Big George into The Space. But another part of him knows Moon is right: It isn't Louie's fault if Big George recognized him. As it happens, Louie does not have time to act on his decision.

It is midday when they hear the first sirens, much closer than they have heard sirens before. Iron, too, seems aware that they are closer, and barks an alarm. Juan and Paco are in the garden; Alf has just run around to the street side with a message for Willie and Moon from Benno. Louie is at his stand at the shuttered front window and Benno is trying to shake him out of the blue funk he has been in.

Suddenly Louie straightens up. "Someone runnin' jus' the other side of the barricade!" Then his voice rises to a near cry. "It Big George. He runnin' fas'. Yeah, that 'im, all right—crazy green hat, stupid shirt. He runnin' like someone chasin' 'im." A pause. Then Louie's voice fills with such pain he can barely whisper. "Someone chasin' him the cops! They gonna foller 'im inta the street. Ozzie! Where are ya!" He leaps away from the window and tears down the stairs for Ozzie, who is in the backyard carrying water to the plants.

Meanwhile Benno dashes to the front. "Ev'ybody in, quick!" he yells. "I mean *quick*!" And the street is full of children running for the safety of the window hatch or for cover in the shadow of the side wall of the house, as Big George scrambles over the barricade and runs toward a pile of rubble.

Most of the kids have made it to the back of the house by the time Big George dashes from his cover, leaps to the front stoop, and starts banging on the boarded-up door. "Lemme in, hey!" he yells. "Louie, open dis door, or ya gonna be sorry!"

Now, over the barricade, spewing pieces of concrete and rubble down its slope, come two policemen, one after the other. "Hold it right there!" the first yells, as he spies Big George on the stoop. Big George freezes and leans on the door, his hands above his head.

Around the side of the house, Moon and Willie are still crouching in the shadow. Getting the little kids in, they were too late to make it to the back window before the police appeared. Out of the corner of an eye, the second policeman sees something.

"I think there are more of them around there," he says.

"Let's get this one, first. He's the kingpin. He's the big Poison. Such a *big man*," he drawls as he ambles over to search Big George. "Look at that!" he says. "Wonder what this can be in this neat little plastic envelope?"

While the second policeman is snapping the cuffs on, Moon gives Willie a prod and they dash for the window under the steps, taking a moment to drag trash and rubble behind them, then closing and locking the wooden hatch. They are shaken and out of breath. In total darkness, they feel their way to the stairway and quietly climb the stairs. They find the others huddled on the floor close to the front window. There isn't a sound in the room.

Through the shutters, much can be seen and heard. The policemen have Big George propped against the barricade and one is standing guard over him. The other now ventures toward the side of the house where he saw the kids.

"They're not here now," he yells. "I'm gonna take a look around the back." He is out of sight, but they can hear him stumbling over unexpected obstacles. Benno crawls to the back window and can see him standing just outside, with hands on his hips, face full of surprise, as he regards the garden. Then he starts a survey of the building from where he stands, letting his eyes trace the whole back, from top to bottom. He looks confused, and in another minute, with a last look at the garden, he disappears around the side and reappears in the front.

"I don't see any way they could get into that house," he says. "It's boarded up tight. Only thing open is a shutter on the second floor and they're not cats. Maybe they aren't in there. But here's the funny thing: There's a garden full of vegetables back there."

"You kiddin' me?" the other policeman says.

"No, honest."

"They've got to be in there, then. How many did you see?"

"I don't know. It was such a quick thing. There could be two or there could be a bunch."

The policeman guarding Big George gives him a shake. "How many of your pals are in there, Georgie?"

They cannot hear Big George's answer, but he seems to be doing a lot of talking.

"He rattin' on us," Louie moans. "I know he rattin' on us."

"They already know we're here, Louie," Benno says. "What kin he tell 'em?"

"Tell 'em we parta the gang."

"Nah, why'd he do that?"

"Maybe they go easy on 'im."

This makes something else for Benno to stew about. His mind goes over and over the possibilities: building more possibilities on possibilities, until he sees the Secret City citizens in a police line-up. So when Louie, once again, says it's all his own fault, Benno is inclined to agree with him—at least one side of his head is.

"We need reinforcements," the first policeman says. "Can't guard this guy and bust that house at the same time." He thinks a moment. "Tell you what. Let's get this guy back to the car and lock him up good. Then you get a blanket, a flashlight, and a thermos from the car and park yourself here until we can get some of the men from the station house out here. Bring your radio-phone and we'll give you a buzz when we're comin' in. In the meantime, keep your hand on your gun, and let 'em have it if they try to move out of there."

"Jeez!" Willie says. "Now they wanna shoot us!" Paco begins to cry; Ozzie has become part of Louie's leg.

As the two policemen and Big George climb the barricade and start their trudge across the obstacle course to the police car, Benno springs into action. "Ev'ybody gotta do somethin' quick, now," he says, "'fore that cop come back. We gonna go out t' the garden an' bring in anything there is what we kin eat. Git it? Now!" And they make for the stairs and out to the garden carrying

179

paper bags and cans and in a matter of minutes have pulled every bean plant and carrot, dug the potatoes, and taken all the apples they can reach; Alf has carefully harvested his little crop of lemon grass which adds such zest to his soups. These are dropped through the basement window. Then, checking to see that the policeman has still not shown up, they take the time to push more rubble around the space under the outside stairway, to conceal the window. And then they are all inside, about to lock the basement hatch, when they realize Iron is not among them. Moon whistles. There are barks, but they are far off. He whistles again.

"We gotta close it," Benno says.

"Not without Iron," Juan pleads.

"We gotta." And they do.

"Now," Benno says, "they know we're here, but they don' know how many, so what we do we gotta do pretty quiet. Firs' thing, we gotta close the back shutter."

"Gonna be so dark," Paco says.

"Dark ain't nothin'," Juan tells him. "Look what we done to our garden!" and his face is stricken. "Such a wonnerful garden."

By the time they have carefully stashed the food in the pantry corner of the basement and collected water for their needs, the young policeman has returned. He arranges his campsite with care, laying an army blanket over a swept part of the street and settling himself in the middle of it. He sets out a small oil lantern, a thermos, and then reaches for his holster and proceeds to check his revolver.

Now, over the rubble behind the barricade other voices can be heard, and then two heads appear around the far end. Benno can't believe it. "Marie and Pete!" he exclaims. "It Marie and Pete."

Everybody crowds to see, disregarding the rule of silence. There they are, and now Benno remembers that this is the day that Marie said she'd try to come. She is talking to the policeman now. "What's going on here?"

"Who are you, lady?" the young policeman asks.

"My name is Marie Lorry. This is Peter Powell. I'm a social counselor at the hospital. He's a reporter. Now, would you be kind enough to tell us what you are doing camped here?" Her voice is courteous but demanding.

"I'm waitin' for reinforcements, miss," the young policeman says.

"Reinforcements for what?"

"We just picked up Big George, the leader of one of the local gangs, and the rest of the bunch is in there. We don't know how many, so we're getting some more men."

Marie looks like she will explode. "These kids are not part of a gang! Where'd you ever get an idea like that?"

"From the guy we collared."

Pete butts in now. "Whoever he is, he's lying or crazy. These are really young kids. The oldest may be thirteen. A couple are maybe six years old."

"There's kids all ages in gangs, today, sir," the policeman says.

"I know these boys, officer," Marie says. "I have an appointment with them here today. There is absolutely nothing that these children are doing that would warrant a police raid. Have you some way to call your station house and call this off? This is ridiculous."

"No, ma'am, not at this range. When they get closer in I can pick 'em up."

Pete says, "Marie, will you feel okay staying here with this officer? I'd like to get to a phone and file this story and see if I can have a remote TV crew standing by. What did you say your name was, officer?"

"Main, sir. Michael C. Main." The policeman looks nervous as Pete starts stumbling his way out of The Space.

Marie walks slowly over to the front of the house and looks up. "I don't know if you can hear me, kids," she calls. They can. "I just want you to know that I'm going to be here every minute until this gets straightened out. Meanwhile, if you hear me, Benno, Moon, can you drop me a note with phone numbers where I can reach your parents to let them know you're okay. I'm going to walk around to the back."

Quickly Benno tears off the edge of a piece of newspaper and writes the number of the phone that is in the hallway of his tenement, and the same for Moon and the cousins. He opens the back window and shutter and drops it down to Marie.

"I'll call them as soon as I see what's going to happen here, or else I'll have Pete do it. Don't worry."

"Thanks, Marie," Benno calls.

The young policeman is getting a call on his police radio. "We're just outside here. I've got six men. We're coming in. Over."

"Hey!" Patrolman Main says. "Don't come in too strong. I got a lady here says she knows these kids."

"Oh yeah? So hold her, too. Over and out."

The swept street is full of policemen stomping about awaiting orders. The south barricade is a shambles from the clambering of so many heavily shod feet.

182

"Lookit the wall!" Juan complains. "Lookit what they done t' our wall." And Benno can only think how much he wishes that that is all that will be done, but in his aching insides he feels that the wall, the garden—those things are the least of it. And so he says "Shut up!" to Juan, and then he shakes his head, and his eyes say to Juan "I didn't mean that."

The policeman in charge is now dispersing the men to all sides of the building. He himself has a bullhorn that he is adjusting.

"They got us surrounded," Willie says. "I don' b'lieve this." Benno wishes he didn't believe it either.

"I'm addressing the occupants of the building," comes the voice of the police officer, sounding like a radio turned up to its highest volume, with a lot of bass in it. "You know we have Big George in custody. He's told us the whole story. We want you to come out now, quietly, with your hands up. Leave any weapons where they are. We're waiting."

"Yeah, like leave the sharp sticks and the slingshots?" Louie mutters. "Man! I'd like to jus' get one good shot at that pigeon Big George."

"We're waiting!" comes the voice on the bullhorn.

No answer comes from the house.

They can see Marie talking to the policeman with the bullhorn. She seems to be getting nowhere: He keeps shaking his head. At one point he raises his voice and he says, "Lady, I can take you in charge for obstructing the police." And Marie replies, "You've seen my credentials. This is going to sound very ugly in court. I am staking my reputation and my job on the fact that these youngsters have nothing whatever to do with any gang."

The policeman seems to be listening now. "Whether

they do or they don't, they can't stay in that house. They're trespassing on city property; they're occupying condemned premises and violating about ten other city ordinances. And I'm going to get them out of there one way or another. So if they don't come out on their own, it's going to be some other way."

And then, suddenly, Pete's back and he isn't alone: He's got some men with electronic equipment and cameras that bear the logo of the city television station. They are standing on the shifting barricade, making hand and arm signals to someone or something that is out of sight. A camera is being set up. Pete moves toward the building, holding a microphone and saying "Testing, testing."

"Jeez," Louie says. "I think we gonna be on TV."

"I think yer right," Benno says. "But why?"

Behind the boarded-up window frame, Benno now tries to pry open the window itself, and with Louie's help they inch it up until they can hear Pete speaking into the microphone below them.

"This is Peter Powell, speaking to you from location in the desolate and rubbled part of the city that you have been reading about in the *City News* and hearing about on this station. The camera is now showing you the house that some young boys, otherwise uncared for and sleeping on city streets, have restored for themselves, turning this derelict building into a comfortable home."

The policemen standing near Pete have stopped patrolling the house and are looking at the television monitor, which shows a close-up of the boarded-up house, then a pan shot over to the swept street, the neat stacks of bricks and building materials, the intact north barricade.

"What you are seeing," Pete continues, "is the handiwork of eight young boys, all under the age of thirteen, one as young as five. They have done this without adult aid. I wish I could show you their vegetable garden, but I understand that they have harvested it quickly to feed themselves now that this house is under seige." Pete takes a breath.

"Yes, I said under seige. The policemen whom you see surrounding this house are attempting to get these children to, quote, surrender. What crime do you think these children have committed that eight policemen are needed to apprehend them? I think I will have Miss Marie Lorry, social counselor, give you a quick rundown on their crimes. Miss Lorry."

The kids are watching the scene below and hearing Pete's broadcast as if they were watching the whole thing on a screen.

"Why don' they show us?" Juan wants to know.

"They can't see us, dummy," Willie says.

Below them, now, the police sergeant in charge is holding up a funny-looking gadget. It looks more like a fire cracker than anything else. Meanwhile one of the officers at the side of the house is yelling, "I swear, sarge, I can't find any way they could get in or out of this place."

"Well, they didn't just drop through the ground," the sergeant calls back.

"I dunno," comes the call from the side. "Maybe they got a bunker. The back yard looks all dug up."

They have missed the beginning of Marie's part in the broadcast, but when the policemen stop yelling, they can hear her saying, "I first met them when they risked the safety of their secret home to bring an old and sick man to the hospital, carrying him over this rough ground on a home-made stretcher." And the camera pans over the desert landscape of The Space.

"Gosh," Moon says, "we soun' like a buncha angels!"

"Little by little I got to know these children and they entrusted me with their secret and allowed me to visit them here. The police you see now are distributing smoke bombs, ladies and gentleman. Smoke bombs! To clear homeless children from the home they've built for themselves."

The police sergeant is called to his radio-phone. He listens for a few moments, then raises his arm. "Chief says hold the smoke, men," he calls. "Okay, kids, I want to give you every chance to get out of there with nobody getting hurt."

"Their crime," Marie goes on, "is hope, ambition, enterprise, independence, concern, aspiration. For that so-called crime, the policemen, here, would like to try to wrench these children from their rehabilitated home, the only home some of them have had for a long time."

Inside the house, while the boys' anxiety about the present is being quieted by the support of Marie and Pete, their concern about their future is rising.

"What they gonna do t' us if they make us git outta here?" Willie asks. But, of course, everyone is worrying about that in his own way.

Pete takes the microphone from Marie. "Marie Lorry happens to be here today because she had previously made an appointment with these children to discuss their present living arrangements and to plan for the future. She arrived to find this forceable eviction in progress. How do you explain to children who have done something heroic, courageous, even pioneering" (Benno smiles) "that it warrants a raid by the police?

"I want to throw in a word here about the city. The city is about to approve the building of middle-income apartments in this area—nothing these street families can afford, even if they spent their entire welfare check for rent, and even if they could get one of the apartments. Who is the most in need of help, right now? That is the question to be answered. We will be taking calls all day, at this station, to hear from concerned residents of this city; from those who want to be heard and from those who want to help. And, Mr. Mayor, if you are listening, we'd like to hear from you and your staff about your ideas of what you can do *now* to help cure one of the most serious problems ever to have hit this city: the homelessness of so many of its people."

The police sergeant is talking on the radio-phone again. He is saying, "Yes, *sir*! Yes, Your Honor!" And then he pushes the phone to Pete. "Hold it, men," the sergeant calls to his officers.

"Yes, Your Honor?" Pete sounds cool, and his side of the conversation is being broadcast. "No, sir, we are acting legally and within our rights to broadcast a live-action outrage like this." He listens for a minute. "Well, you see, Your Honor, we—Marie Lorry and I—have been working out the details of a plan for some nights now, along with some influential people in this city, and we now have a proposal that could get good-quality, very low cost housing into this big area in the shortest possible time. And not only houses—all the support systems needed—schools, a hospital, a halfway facility." Pause. "Yes, sir, I know it takes money, but already we have received substantial pledges, along with generous offers of volunteer labor and materials. Pledges are coming in as we speak. If the city can match what we raise this way, and the plan we have arrived at can get your approval and cooperation, this is going to reflect magnificently upon your administration. The influential people I mentioned, many of whom, I might say, are your supporters, will be in touch about details. Our private commission will begin at once, in any case. This is a very important decision for you, Mr. Mayor, and for the city at large. I'll hand you back to the police, sir."

Pete can be seen talking with Marie. It seems to take forever for him to tell her everything. She's smiling.

In the house, the children's eyes have not left the drama for a moment.

"Ya theenk po-lice gonna leave, ever een de world?" Alf asks, his enormous dark eyes looking watery and weary. "I never been nowhere where people like us mix wif po-lice and we ween, eef po-lice wants sometheeng differnt." And he takes out the little true bone and starts marking in the dust on the floor.

"What it say?" Ozzie asks.

"True bone don' work good here, now," Alf says. "True bone ees meex-up. Too much bad een air now." He pockets it and erases the markings on the floor.

Marie is calling to them. "Kids, Pete and I are coming around. Will you let us in? The police are pulling out for now, except for two of them to patrol."

They dive for the basement to let Marie and Pete in through the locked hatch. They are welcomed as heroes.

"Let's go sit down and powwow," Marie says. Benno laughs. "Alf," Marie goes on, "do you have any more of

188

those little corn cakes? I'm starved. And I'll drink a sip of water, too, if you have some to spare."

In minutes they are sitting around the fireplace, munching corn cakes, apples, sipping water. "Before I forget, Benno, Moon, Juan, Paco—we got calls through to your families. They know you're safe and that you may not be home until late, or even until tomorrow. I wasn't sure we'd be able to talk those officers out of it and I thought they might hold you here overnight, or for days." Benno had thought that, too. He had thought they might be surrounded by cops with revolvers, even shooting it out in the end—an uneven fight of bullets against pointed sticks and slingshots. So *that* fear is over. But what next?

"I can't possibly tell you all about it. It would take too long. But here is what has happened, and here is what we expect to happen. A private commission has been set up. Pete and I and a very experienced man are heading it. The purpose will be to do something very much like what you and I talked about, Benno. Remember? We will rebuild this area with the help of professionals, volunteers, residents who will actually be living here, the national guard, if need be, army engineers, if we can't get enough private assistance. We have architects volunteering already; we have skilled craftsmen volunteering hours. And we'll go after city-owned buildings in other areas, too."

"I volunteer," Benno says.

"Me, too," Moon says.

"I'm going to need you," Marie says. "Every day after school, I'm going to need you." Benno cannot believe his luck. He is going to work with this beautiful person to help make everything they want to happen come true in The Space.

"Now we have to get the city's cooperation to let us use all the available city-owned derelict buildings. That's Pete's job, and he's got the paper and the TV station behind him."

"An' we jus' gonna go on livin' here, right?" Willie asks.

Marie frowns. "Now let me tell you the solution to that problem. You have to understand you can't. It's known you are here in an unsafe, illegal way. The city is going to put you out, one way or another, and a really good alternative is the way we have already thought out for you, and I think you will agree. So be patient and listen to me, please."

Pete says, "Marie's been working twenty-four hours a day on this, talking to everyone with influence in the city. If anyone can get this done, she can, and I want you to know that her first interest is that you each be settled happily somewhere."

"We happy here," Alf mourns.

Marie reaches out and pats his shoulder. "Just listen," she says. "You may all stay here tonight, if you wish. You may want to talk, get your things together, even have a party! Now, one by one. Benno and Moon will be returning to their families, but, as I said, they will be working for our commission, which, incidentally, we still have to name. Louie, your mother is being discharged from the hospital; your baby sister is already with her. Your mother is being given train fare to your grandmother's home down south, with tickets for you and Ozzie. Now, they made a mistake. They put a ticket in for the baby, but she travels free, so there's an extra ticket. Louie's mother says she's so grateful for what you boys have all done together, she would gladly take one of you with her. Does anyone have any ideas on that?"

There's silence for a bit. Everyone is looking at everyone else. Then Louie says, "Well, I tell ya, Willie an' me, we git on real good inna alley. Maybe if he wanna come. . . ?"

"Willie," Marie asks, "what do you think?"

Willie is so surprised he is speechless at first. Here he's been welcomed into two families, so to speak, within only a few months, when his life before that was that of an outcast. "I'll go wit ya, Louie. Trut' is, I ruther be inna city wit all these frien's, but it gonna git cold onna street agin."

"Yeah, but listen, Willie," Louie says. "Maybe nex' year, after my ma and the kids is all settle down south, maybe you and me kin come back wit the projec' an' help, like Moon an' Benno." Willie grins. How come he has turned lucʰv? he wonders.

"Okay," Marie says, smiling at them. "Now Juan and Paco. Your mother is going to start working in the linen room at the hospital, part time. We're seeing to it that she gets housing close by. So that's set."

Paco says, "Hear that, Juan? We gonna have our own place. I gonna have a garden inna window."

Alf has been sitting huddled and shivering in a corner. Nobody has mentioned what is to happen to him. A great circle of loneliness has put cold arms around him. But Marie has not forgotten him.

"Now Alf," she says. She is smiling, but she has a shy, almost nervous look about her. "Alf, if you'd like it, I'd like very, very much for you to come and stay with me.

191

What would you think of that?" She looks so concerned. He may refuse her.

"Wif you, Mees Marie!"

"With me," she says, her face hopeful. She knows there are months of redtape and paperwork to make this happen, but for now . . . All Alf does is pick up his stuff and move over and sit close beside her. He doesn't say a word, and he doesn't ask the true bone the answer.

seventeen

*Above the City is the same sky
that covers the whole world.*

It takes them a little while to absorb everything that has happened this day—this incredibly long and active day: the pursuit and capture of Big George; the threat by the police to their homestead; their story on TV; the great plan of Marie and Pete's; the promise of a future for The Space; and finally, a home and hope for all of these pioneers.

And so they are silent for a while, or else, like Ozzie, exhausted from so much going on, curled for a nap. But finally Alf says, "I got a beeg pail boileen to make de las' good soup. Ev'ytheen go eenta eet. We got de las' corn cakes and I musheen up some apples to make a kinda jam. We goeen to have a party."

So, an hour later, when the soup is done—hot and tangy with its lemon grass, thickened with the potatoes, interesting with the carrots and beans and rice—they all dig in as if it is their last supper because it is their last supper. Sadness is moderated by the excitement offered by the future. When was it that any of these children could look ahead? Anticipatory pleasure is a new experience for most of them. It is an unknown luxury.

And when the food has disappeared and there is not even a crumb left for the resident mice, two things happen. First: They remember Iron. "Iron!" Willie cries. "Where he been all day?" He runs to the back window to look. Iron is not there; only the tumbled garden with its slightly smoking cooking pit where Alf cooked the soup. It looks abandoned and sad. Then quickly to the front window. "Aha!" Willie laughs. "Lookit 'im!" There, in the failing light, the two policemen on guard are camped on a blanket, lit by the light of two oil lanterns. But they are sitting very, very still. Over these guards stands the guard of them all—old Iron—keeping them still as statues.

"I don' think the po-lice gonna bother us none t'night." Louie laughs. He is surprised by the sound of his own laugh. Had he forgotten how for a while?

Now Willie suddenly twists himself onto his back and, whistling through his teeth, starts doing a little break dancing on the floor. Alf dives into his pocket, comes out with a rubber band stretched over a bent piece of metal, and starts twanging it against his teeth. Louie pulls his comb out and starts humming into it. Ozzie, Juan, and Paco just dance around like puppets, while Moon and Benno clap and hum. They can hear Iron making throaty sounds.

"He singin' 'long," Willie says. "Good ol' Iron. Gonna miss 'im. Hey! What gonna happen t' Iron?" The show stops.

"He stay here, he gonna be a wild dog again or he

gonna be et up by a wild dog," Louie says. "Maybe he kin go sout' wit us an' be our houn' dog."

"Me, I like Iron," Alf says. "Maybe Marie take me an' Iron, too."

"Know what I think?" Benno says. "I think he b'long wit McWhat. I think Iron gonna like that, and I think McWhat gonna like it, too. We gotta ask Marie 'bout that."

Then, spending their first night in the house, Benno, Moon, Juan, and Paco join the others who are sleeping their last night in the old house. "Maybe," Willie says, "we come back and we work on this house, ourselfs, an' make it fer us again. Or anyway, we find a other an' . . ." And they are all asleep.

In the morning, Marie and Pete are there to awaken them and give them thermoses of orange juice and hot cocoa. "It's not corn cakes, but it'll have to do until Alf shows me how to make those," she says, laughing.

"Marie," Benno says. "Member ya said the commission fer The Space has t' have a name?"

"Yes, it does," Marie says, helping them fold up their blankets. "And incidentally, kids, the people who will care for Mr. McWhat will let him have his dog with him. How's that?"

"Terrific!" Moon says. "Terrific!"

Benno is still trying to call her attention to what's on his mind. "Marie," he tries again, "because Moon and me, we discover The Space, ya think ya could let him an' me give all this a name? We can't go on callin' it Secret City. It ain't a secret nomore."

"If you've got a good idea, I guess we could try to

push it through. Anyhow, I can give you the right to name the commission."

Benno takes Moon aside and signs with him for a little while. Moon is nodding agreeably. "Okay," Benno says, "we got a name. We gonna make a sign on a piecea board with a marker. That okay?" Marie nods.

Now, outside, there seems to be a gathering. There's the whole TV crew again, and Pete with his microphone. Juan yells, "Hey, look! There Tio Chico! He finally git up here! Ain't that Benno's ma and pa? Ain't that his brother?"

Marie looks out the window, annoyed. "That's Pete, all right, going to get everything he can out of it. But why not? We'll get some more contributions for our great new space. Right? Okay, let's go, friends."

Down the stairs they go, for the last time, and across the dark cellar, where the water supply and pantry were once their lifeline. Then out the window hatch and into the jumbled yard where little children had made things grow. Around the side of the house they troop, appearing one by one: Louie first, with Ozzie close behind, clinging to his shirttail. A cheer goes up and Louie's face shows surprise and pleasure. He thrusts both arms in the air and clasps one hand with the other. Then he brings his arms down and throws one around Ozzie. Next comes Willie, then Juan and Paco, then Alf leading Iron. And all are greeted by applause that makes them beam and laugh.

"Hey, we're really on TV," Paco exclaims. "We're stars!"

"You're a star, all right, kid," Pete calls from his place at the microphone. "You're all stars. Ladies and gentlemen gathered here today, and those of you in your

196

comfortable homes watching this telecast—when you have seen what these children have done, by themselves, with only their aspirations, without the aid of tools, can you *imagine* what we can do with an organization with aspirations *and* tools and your support!"

There are still two more pioneers to emerge from the shadows of the side wall, and now they come—Benno and Moon, a large flat board held above their heads, big smiles on their faces.

JOJO'S SPACE

reads the sign.

Benno thinks he sees the little man with the beret in the crowd, but he disappears so quickly he can't be sure. It's funny, though, he never saw him in The Space before.

City asleep
City asleep
Papers fly at the garbage heap.
Refuse dumped and
The sea gulls reap
Grapefruit rinds
And coffee grinds.
The sea gull reels and
The field mouse steals
In for a bite
At the end of the night
Of crusts and crumbs
And pits of plums.
The white eggshells
And the green-blue smells
And the gray gull's cry
And the red dawn sky . . .
City asleep
City asleep
A carnival
On the garbage heap.

"City-Dump" by Felice Holman
first published in *At the Top of My Voice
and Other Poems* © 1970